THE H ꜱ
AWAKENING

HELEN PRYKE

Print ISBN 978-1-913942-11-3

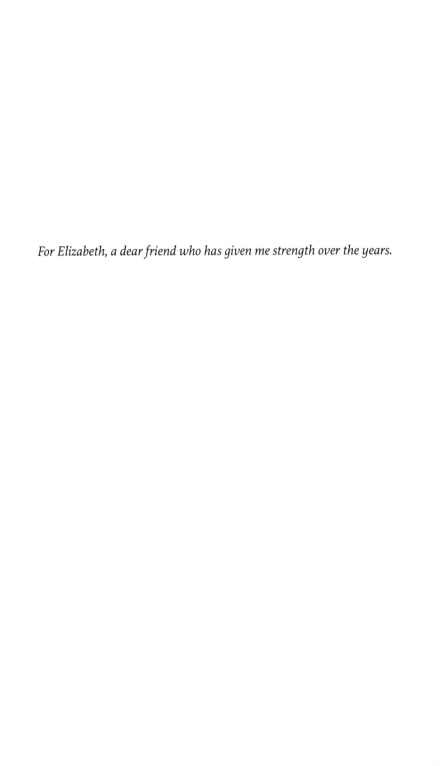

For Elizabeth, a dear friend who has given me strength over the years.

TUSCANY, 1844

L ucrezia crouched behind the sofa, clutching her doll to her chest, as her father's voice grew louder and angrier. Her heart thumped so hard, she was sure they would hear it and drag her out from her hiding place. A small whimper escaped her throat, and she froze in fear.

'I will not have commoners from the valley coming to you for your remedies, Ginevra, as if you were a peasant woman desperate to feed her brood of urchins. You are an Innocenti, for pity's sake! We do not sell potions to all and sundry.'

'I have never asked them for money, I swear.' Lucrezia could imagine her mother standing with her head bowed, her eyes on the floor as she searched for the right words to placate her husband. 'They bring me gifts to thank me, that is all it is. I-I want to help them, give them medicines that will cure their children's coughs and maladies, or give an elderly relative the strength to carry on. Simple things that make their lives better.'

'Simple things? Simple!' Papà's scorn echoed around the room, filling every crevice, ringing in Lucrezia's head. 'Do you know what they're calling you? Do you? Oh yes, the ones you help, the *peasants* in the villages, they say you're a wise woman, a sage, a *healer*…' He spat the word as if it were poison. 'Others call you a witch, a heretic, a blasphemer, an atheist – those are the kinder ones. There's talk in the town of having the priest come here to purge you of your sins and the evil spirits within you. They want me to throw you in the asylum.'

Mamma gasped. 'No, Ludovico! That can't be. I use the plants in the Grove to make medicines, as my family has done for generations. No one has ever accused us of doing wrong.'

'Really? Wasn't one of your ancestors burned at the stake?'

Lucrezia thrust her hand into her mouth and bit down to stop herself from crying out. She had heard the story about Morgana Innocenti from tales her grandmother used to tell. The old woman's mind had gone by then, and she would recount stories of people long dead, her face animated as she spoke, heedless of the nightmares that would visit her granddaughter for many nights after.

'She wasn't a witch. None of us are witches. We're healers.'

Lucrezia could hear a defiant tone creeping into Mamma's voice, and shook her head, willing her mother to stop. She could picture Papà's face, a black cloud descending over him as the anger built up at her mother's insolence.

There was a loud crack, and a startled cry from Ginevra. Lucrezia crept forward and peered round the edge of the sofa. Mamma sat on the floor, her hand pressed against the side of her face, tears streaming down her cheeks. Papà crouched down and grasped a clump of her hair in his hand.

'It stops, now. No more potions, no more medicines, and no more Grove. The cottage will be closed up and no one will be allowed to go there anymore. I will not have the whole valley talk about my wife as if she were some sort of sorceress. Do you understand?'

Lucrezia saw Mamma nod slowly. Papà held his hand out and helped her to her feet.

'We shall speak no more of this nonsense. You will confess your sins to Don Andrea and be cleansed of them, and this ridiculous tradition will end here.'

Mamma's hands dropped to her sides, and Lucrezia could see the livid red mark Papà had left on her cheek.

'This is for the best, Ginevra. Our daughter's name will be sullied by your behaviour if it continues. She's only four, such a tender age. I'm sure you wouldn't want to see any harm come to her, would you? Considering I know I didn't actually father her, my *faithful* Ginevra.' This last was said with a hiss, a terrible sneer on his face. He held out his hand, and after a moment's hesitation, she took it. He pulled her close to him and kissed her fiercely.

Lucrezia could see Mamma's expressionless green eyes, devoid of any emotion, staring into the empty space behind Papà. Then her mother turned her head slightly and stared straight at her, and a tiny spark of defiance lit up her face. Lucrezia gasped and shuffled backwards until she could no longer see her parents, her cheeks burning with shame and... something else. She thought for a moment, then realised what it was. Fear.

1

JANUARY 1880

Sara's boots made a crunching sound as they broke through the crisp surface of the snow that had fallen a couple of days earlier. All around her was an eerie silence, every noise muffled by the icy blanket that covered the ground. She was at the edge of the woods; to go any further was forbidden. She knew her mother would be angry if she found out, and hesitated.

There it was again! A flash of brilliant blue as the dragonfly darted among the snow-laden branches, going deeper into the woods. Sara had followed it up to here, amazed at finding the insect this time of year. She looked around, checking to see if any of the servants were nearby, then headed into the woods after her new-found friend. She went further in than she'd ever been before, causing her to have a moment of panic as she wondered how she'd ever find her way back to the villa. Glancing behind her, she saw her footprints clear and crisp across the snow, and thanked God under her breath.

She ducked beneath a branch, gasping as some snow slid off and hit the back of her neck. She shook the collar of her woollen coat, trying to dislodge the snow, and shivered as some of it slithered down her back. The dragonfly darted back and forth between her and a clearing up ahead, its agitated movements urging her on.

'All right, all right, I'm coming,' she muttered, stamping her feet to bring some warmth back into her toes. 'You don't have to worry about getting cold and wet, flying around like that!'

Sara broke through the last of the trees and stood in the middle of the clearing. She was surprised to see a stone-walled cottage before her, the late-afternoon sun glinting dully off its grimy windows. The cottage had an air of neglect and abandonment about it, as if no one had been there for years. She walked up to the door and reached out to open it, expecting it to be locked. As soon as she touched the knob, it was as though a bolt of lightning shot up her arm. She snatched her hand away and rubbed her tingling fingers, trembling as an image – *a woman in the kitchen, stirring a bubbling pot over the fire, the aroma of herbs wafting through the cottage as she sang quietly* – flashed through her mind. Bewildered, Sara took a step back, cradling her hand close to her chest.

She jumped as the dragonfly returned, passing so close to her face that she could feel the air vibrating from its wings. It circled her head a few times, then took off in a straight line in the opposite direction. Sara followed it, glad to get away from the cottage. She could sense it behind her, silent and empty, as though judging her worthiness to be there.

The dragonfly headed down through the garden, and Sara stumbled through the snow after it until she arrived at a wooden gate in the middle of a thick, overgrown hedge. She flexed her fingers, relieved that the numbness was wearing off, and pushed the gate open.

She found herself in an enclosed part of the garden, the uneven thick blanket of snow hiding whatever was planted here, although she could see parts of bushes poking through its surface every now and then. She guessed from the bumps in the snow interspersed with flatter areas that it was likely a vegetable garden, with paths running between the rows of plants. Her eyes followed the dragonfly, a dazzling blue flash against the stark white of the snow, and then she noticed the fountain. It was oddly bare of snow, the veined white marble almost camouflaged against the background. There was no water flowing through it, and as she got closer she saw a web of cracks across the surface of the basin. The dragonfly rested on the marble rim, its wings outstretched. Sara sat down, taking care not to startle it, and gazed around her. There was a brick wall on one side, lined with what appeared to be fruit trees, while the other three sides were enclosed by the hedge.

Sara turned to the dragonfly. 'Why did you bring me here?'

It continued to stare at her, its bulbous black eyes glittering in the last rays of sunlight. She found she couldn't tear her eyes away, captured by the pull of its gaze. Images flashed through her mind, a confused jumble of vague faces and blurry scenes that gradually became clearer. A shadowy figure appeared, walking through the garden, heedless of the snow that covered the ground. As it drew closer, Sara saw it was a woman, dressed in an old-fashioned tunic, her dark curls falling around her face as she bent down to caress a plant. She lifted her head and smiled at Sara, then turned as another woman walked towards them. And another. The garden was soon filled with women, so insubstantial that Sara could see the snow-covered plants and trees through their bodies. She clasped her hands together, hardly daring to move, as they turned to look at her. And then they were gone, as abruptly as a candle being extinguished.

Sara slowly stood, stretching her back as she wondered what she had just seen. The sun had almost disappeared behind the mountains, and she shivered, the damp cold suddenly seeping into her bones. She looked for the dragonfly, but it had gone.

Realising she was alone, she got up and hurried out of the garden, carefully closing the gate behind her. She took a final look around and vowed to come back when the snow had melted, to see what was hidden below its surface.

She headed back towards the cottage, wondering who had once lived there and why it was abandoned now. When she arrived at the door, she couldn't resist peeking into the nearby window. Her eyes took a little time to adjust to the gloomy interior, but once they had, she could see an open fireplace, a wooden table, and pots hanging from hooks on the walls.

The image came, unbidden, into her mind of the woman standing over the fire, stirring the pot as she hummed quietly to herself. The hem of her plain brown linen dress brushed across the tiles on the floor, her slim shape outlined by the material. Her auburn hair, with bright red strands that glinted when they caught the light, was loosely tied in a plait; the woman wiped her hand across her brow and brushed away some tendrils that had escaped. She put the spoon down on the hearth, dipped her finger into the pot and tasted whatever had been cooking, then turned around with a smile.

Sara gasped when she saw the woman's startling green eyes, even brighter than her own. She backed away from the house, turned, and ran as quickly as she could, stumbling in the deep drifts of snow as she fled.

2

Sara sneaked in the side entrance, quietly shutting the door behind her as she looked around for servants, and hung her coat up in the cloakroom. She crept into the kitchen and went over to the fire, leaving a damp trail on the floor. The snow had leaked through her boots and her feet were frozen. Her fingers, numb from the cold, fumbled with the laces, and she pulled her boots off with some difficulty. She kicked them as close to the fire as possible, then removed her sopping wet stockings and hung them over the back of a chair. Sitting down, she stretched out her feet towards the crackling flames and rested them on the brick hearth, sighing as warmth flooded back into her toes.

'Lady Sara, your mother has been calling you for the last half an hour,' came a voice from the other side of the kitchen. Sara sat up with a groan, unwilling to give up her warm spot just yet.

Rosa, once Sara's nanny and now her mother's most trusted servant, strode over and stood before her, eyes wide open at the sight of Sara's wet clothes. '*Mio Dio*, you must get changed at once. You'll catch your death if not. I'll send Sofia to help you.

Go, go, and I'll tell the contessa you're home. She's in the drawing room. When you're ready, go there and I'll bring you a nice hot cup of tea and something to eat.'

Sara hesitated, still reluctant to leave the snug kitchen and go up to her icy cold room.

'Shoo now,' Rosa insisted. 'You've got to get out of those damp clothes. Here, put these on.' She handed her a pair of felt slippers.

Knowing it was pointless arguing, Sara put on the slippers and used the chair to pull herself up. The cold tiled floor made her shiver.

'All right, I'm going,' she said as she saw Rosa open her mouth to tell her off once again. She wrapped her arms around her body, trying to retain some heat, and ran through the house up to her room.

Twenty minutes later, she entered the drawing room, dressed in dry clothes. A small fire crackled in the grate, barely warming the enormous space. Sara often wondered why her mother insisted on using this room in the winter, when there were many smaller, more comfortable rooms that would be a lot easier to heat. She saw the contessa in her usual armchair, dressed in her customary dark grey dress, a velvet choker around her long, slender neck, her face pale against her black hair scraped into a tight bun. The small flecks of emerald green in her hazel brown eyes that would sparkle when she became angry, or on those rare occasions she laughed, were the only hint of colour in her otherwise severe appearance.

She suppressed a sigh and went over to her mother. 'Good evening, Mamma.' Sara put on her most winsome smile, hoping her mother hadn't noticed her tardiness. Another of her many rules was to always be home by the time night fell, especially in winter.

Her mother pursed her lips. 'I've been waiting for over an hour, Sara. Where have you been?'

Sara lowered her eyes to the floor. 'I-I was in the kitchen. I was hungry, and asked Rosa to make me something. I'm sorry I'm so late.'

Her mother's silk dress rustled as she stood, her face white with anger. A resounding crack resonated around the room. Sara staggered backwards, too shocked to cry out, her hand cradling her flaming cheek that Lucrezia had struck. She was sure there were angry red welts there, left by her mother's bony fingers.

'Liar! Rosa told me she sent you upstairs to change your clothes because you were soaking wet. I repeat, where have you been?'

'I-I went for a walk, out in the snow. My boots and stockings were drenched, I was trying to dry them off by the fire in the kitchen.'

'Why did you lie to me? Couldn't you have told me that from the beginning? You must have gone for a long walk to get so cold and wet.'

Sara nodded. Her face tingled, and she knew her voice would tremble if she spoke.

'Come, sit, and tell me about it.' Her mother sank back down into her armchair and gestured to the divan opposite.

Sara sat, composing herself as she had been taught. Being the contessa's daughter meant long days spent learning ridiculous rules, behaving properly, and minding her manners in front of their distinguished guests. Not that there were so many nowadays, not since Papà had started travelling so often and all Mamma's time was taken up with overseeing the running of the estate.

Sara looked up and caught her mother watching her, eyes narrowed, as if trying to read her thoughts. She shuddered and moved closer to the fire in an effort to keep the cold air seeping into her body at bay.

'You went into the woods, didn't you?'

'No! Of course not.'

'Another lie.' Her mother sighed. 'Where did we go wrong with you? Your papà will be so disappointed. One of the gardeners said he saw you heading off into the trees, but he was too far away to stop you.'

Damn servants. First Rosa, then this. Sara clenched her fists. Sometimes being a noble was so... suffocating. Frustrating. Restrictive. She longed for the day when she would be the contessa, then she could do what she wanted. She shoved the thought out of her mind, knowing it could only happen if her parents died. And as harsh as they were with her, she didn't wish for that to happen.

'There was a dragonfly–' she said, but her mother interrupted her.

'What? At this time of year? Don't be ridiculous. Do I have to beat you to stop you lying? My goodness, you're sixteen years old, but you behave like a spoiled little child. I thought I'd brought you up better than that.'

There came a knock at the door and Rosa entered, carrying a tray. 'I've brought you some tea and biscuits,' she said, glancing from Sara to her mother.

'Put it over there and leave us,' the contessa snapped. 'And don't let us be disturbed again.'

Rosa put down the tray and curtsied before leaving the room, closing the door quietly behind her.

Sara waited as her mother poured the tea, murmuring a polite thank you as she took the cup.

'Now, tell me the truth,' her mother said, taking a delicate sip, her gentle tone belying the hard line of her pursed lips.

'There *was* a dragonfly.' Sara rested her cup and saucer on her lap. 'I thought it was strange too, at this time of year, but it was definitely there. I followed it into the woods, I wanted to see if there were more.'

'And were there?' Her mother's expression was carefully neutral, as if she didn't want to show any emotion at all.

'No.' Sara hesitated. 'But I did find a cottage.'

'A cottage?'

Was it Sara's imagination or was her mother's hand trembling? 'Yes, in the middle of a clearing. It looked like no one had lived there for a long time. I wanted to go in, but...' She was suddenly reluctant to tell her mother about the vision she'd had. 'The door was locked, so I looked around the garden.'

'Go on.'

This time there was no mistaking the sound of the cup rattling against the saucer. Sara was mystified. A thought flitted through her mind: *Don't tell her about the garden with the fountain.* She swallowed, unwilling to lie once again to her mother, but she knew that she had to if she ever wanted to go back to the cottage again.

'There isn't really much to tell. Everything was covered in snow, and I didn't want to get any wetter than I already was. It was getting late, too, so I hurried back.'

'And the dragonfly?'

'Gone. I couldn't see it anywhere, I've no idea where it went.' She paused. 'But, Mamma, why is there a cottage in the woods? Who used to live there?'

Her mother shifted in her chair. 'It's very old and falling to pieces. I think the last people who lived there had to move out because it had become dangerous.'

'Who were they?' Sara insisted.

'Only some servants who used to work here. It was a long time ago, nothing that concerns us. So, tell me, how did you find your way back?'

'I followed my footprints in the snow. I'd left a clear trail, thank goodness, otherwise I might have got lost.' Sara shuddered at the thought of being out alone, at night, in those cold, dark woods.

'Let that be a lesson for you,' her mother said sternly. 'There is a reason why I forbid you to go into the woods, it's easy to lose your way out there. My mother...' She paused, then shook her head. 'It doesn't matter. You must never go in the woods again, do you hear me? And I shall tell your father what you have done today. He will want to speak to you.'

'Yes, Mamma,' Sara replied demurely. It was obvious her mother didn't want to talk about the cottage, and she was determined to find out why.

3

MARCH 1880

The snow didn't clear until mid-March. Sara decided that when she wasn't studying or learning how a contessa should behave, she would go to the library and search for books about the history of her family and home. She'd always loved spending time there, and at a young age had vowed to read as many of the books as she could. The shelves were crammed with leather-bound volumes, some so old that little clouds of dust flew out when she opened them, others newer, the leather still stiff and shiny.

There was no time like the present. The house was silent, as if holding its breath in those last moments of calm before the servants arose and began their daily chores. Dawn was breaking, the sky a mix of oranges, pinks and reds. Sara went over to the large French doors and pulled the heavy velvet curtain aside so she could see better. The remnants of a pale mist hung over the perfectly mown lawn that sloped down the hill to the woods beyond. She could see the pond Mamma had had installed years earlier, the water reflecting the incredible colours of the sky. A couple of solitary ducks paddled across it, dabbling their beaks under the water, and ruffling their wings. Sara wondered where the herons were; they had arrived a couple of years ago, and were now permanent fixtures of the pond.

The pond's still waters were calming, and Sara often went there with a blanket, a book, and some stale bread for the ducks. She looked forward to going there again once the weather turned warmer and reading her book, with the sounds of squabbling among the ducks in the background. She sighed; for now, she had a long, boring task ahead of her.

She started from the wall nearest the door and worked her way around the room, as always marvelling at the books on the shelves. The hours passed, but she couldn't find any about the cottage, the Innocenti or their centuries-old villa. What she did find was something she'd seen every day of her life without taking much notice of it – a portrait on the wall, between two bookcases, of her grandmother, Ginevra Innocenti, standing beside a dapple-grey horse, both holding their heads in the same regal pose. She vaguely remembered her grandmother, who'd died when Sara was little, and could see her own features in Ginevra's face; the same shape of the cheekbones, and the freckled, pointy nose and green eyes that she thought made her look like an elf.

She reached out and brushed her fingertips across the surface, following the contours of the brushstrokes, and wished she'd had the chance to know her grandmother. Instead, she only had fleeting memories of comforting embraces as Ginevra softly sang lullabies, and drifting off to sleep with the scent of lavender, rosemary, sage, and other sweet perfumes enveloping her.

The bell for lunch rang in the distance. Sara left the library, disappointed she hadn't found anything. After she had eaten, she asked Rosa about the portrait, but the servant merely told her that her grandmother could ride any horse born then bustled away, mumbling about some bread in the oven that would surely burn if she stayed there chatting idly any longer. Sara stamped her foot in frustration. Why would no one talk to her?

❧

When her father returned from his business trip he gave her a lengthy lecture, as she'd expected. He rarely disciplined her, leaving that task to her mother, which made his words all the more effective when he did. She'd grown up knowing she had already disappointed him by being born a female, especially when no more children had arrived after her, and couldn't bear to see that disapproving look on his face.

'I know what it's like to be young and headstrong, but you must obey your mother on this matter, Sara,' he said. 'Lucrezia has a lot to cope with, and hasn't got time to be watching you as well. The rules she has put in place are for your own good, both now and when you will be the contessa. It is very disappointing when you misbehave like this, after everything we do for you.'

'I'm sorry, Papà.' Sara hung her head, her eyes cast down to the floor. She tried to feel ashamed of her behaviour, but the rebellious streak inside her refused to be quashed.

'The cottage is out of bounds, do you understand?'

Sara nodded meekly.

'It's a dangerous place, no one has been there for years. It could fall down at any moment.'

'Yes, Papà.' Sara didn't think it had looked dangerous at all; in fact, it had looked like it could remain standing for many more centuries, but she didn't dare contradict her father. A feeling of doubt rose in her mind, and she wondered why they were lying to her.

'You must do as you're told, Sara. I haven't taken my belt to you since you were little, but I will do it if I find out you've been there again.'

Sara's breath caught in her throat. She remembered the day well; she'd been no more than six when she'd gone into her mother's room and pulled out all the boxes from her wardrobe, delighted to see what treasures she could find. Her mother had walked in as Sara was standing in front of the mirror, admiring herself in a sable fur coat, jewelled necklaces draped all over her body, a long peacock feather stuck in her hair. Her mother's scream of fury had made Sara wet herself, soiling the silk scarves and leather handbags strewn on the floor around her. She'd never gone into her mother's room again without permission. It had been several days before she was able to sit down properly, and the bruises from the belt had lasted for much longer, turning all colours of the rainbow before slowly disappearing.

Despite her father's threats, once the lecture was over, she was more determined than ever to discover whatever she could about her family. She would just be more careful.

One morning, downhearted after a fruitless search, she went to the stables. No snow had fallen for the last week or so, but the ground was still covered in its frozen white blanket. The sun's rays shone weakly through the clouds, barely warming the icy air. Sara pulled her hat further down onto her head, grateful for its fur lining.

The horses snorted as she approached, looking eagerly over the stable doors to see if she'd brought them anything. She grabbed a handful of carrots from a nearby bucket and handed one to each horse, their velvety muzzles tickling her palm as they gently took the delicacy.

'Good morning, Bernardo,' she said when she reached the last stall. The groom looked up from the hoof he was checking. His leathery skin crinkled around his soft brown eyes as he smiled at her, his black hair heavily sprinkled with grey, his large, capable hands calloused from working with horses for so many years. Sara had been coming to the stables since she was a little girl, and considered Bernardo a dear friend. He was always respectful, like the other servants at the villa, but took the time to stop and chat to her, and often made her laugh.

'Lady Sara, you startled me.'

'Is he all right?' she asked. Apollo, a magnificent black stallion, was her favourite, even though she wasn't allowed to ride him. *So many things are forbidden to me*, she thought, suddenly angry.

Bernardo stood up and patted the horse's neck. 'He was limping this morning. I'm checking his hooves for stones.'

'Please, carry on, don't let me stop you.' Sara watched as he ran his hand down the stallion's leg, clicking his tongue, and tugged its fetlock. Apollo obediently lifted his leg, and Bernardo rested it on his thigh while he used a hoof pick to clean out the dirt and debris.

'Here's the bugger,' he exclaimed, and held up a sharp pointed stone. 'Wedged right down near the frog, must have been bloody painful. Poor devil.' The stallion snorted and shook his head.

'He must be glad that's out,' Sara remarked.

'I s'pose it's like having a toothache. He'll do better now. Did you want something, Lady Sara?'

She realised she was keeping him from his duties. 'Oh no, I came down here for a walk and something to do. I'm tired of being cooped up indoors, and at least the sun's out today. Can I brush one of the ponies?'

'You know your mother would have a fit if she found out you help me with the horses.'

Sara crossed her arms and pouted.

He laughed and tossed her a stiff-bristled brush. 'All right, you win. Ol' Ester down there had a good roll in the mud yesterday, if you want to sort her out.'

Sara spent the next couple of hours brushing the caked-on mud off Ester until her coat gleamed. She finished combing the knots out of the pony's tail and stood back, satisfied with her work.

'You've done a grand job, Lady Sara,' Bernardo said, leaning on the stable door. 'That'll teach the mucky bugger to roll in puddles!'

'She looks a lot better, doesn't she?' Sara looked down at her dusty clothes. 'I'll have to go and get changed, Mamma wants me on time for lunch today. We have visitors.'

'Ah, yes. The duke and his wife. The contessa told me yesterday to be ready when their carriage arrives. You'd best not be late.'

'I'd much rather spend the day here with the horses, they're less trouble.' Sara sighed deeply. Then she had a sudden thought. Maybe Bernardo could answer some of her questions. 'I've heard my grandmother was an excellent rider,' she said casually.

'You've heard right. There was no one better. She could have ridden Apollo bareback, with a side saddle, any way she wanted. She was fearless, and could tame any high-spirited animal. She had a way with horses, that's for sure.'

'Did you know her?' Sara tried to keep her face neutral, afraid he would see her interest and refuse to say any more, as Rosa had. For some reason, no one would speak about her grandmother, which only served to make her all the more curious.

'I was a mere lad when I first met her, a lowly stable boy newly arrived, and I was terrified of the enormous brutes. She saw me hesitate to go and muck out a stable, and told me off. She said the horses would kick out at me – not because they didn't like me, mind, but because they could sense my fear. She showed me how to approach them like I meant business, and she was right. They calmed down and accepted me, and I never had any more problems. You take after her in that, you've an inborn confidence around the horses.'

Sara tutted when she heard Rosa calling her in the distance.

'I've got to go,' she said, reluctant to leave just as Bernardo had started talking to her.

'Why don't you come back tomorrow. I'll tell you some more about your grandmother. I've got a lot of stories about her, she was a wonderful woman and a powerful healer.'

'Healer?'

'Go on with you now, otherwise Rosa will lose her voice,' he said with a laugh. 'I'll tell you more tomorrow.'

Sara took off at a run, gathering her skirts so she could move more quickly. She felt light-headed at the thought that perhaps she would at last learn something about her grandmother.

4

Sara woke up the next morning, excited at the thought of what she might find out that day. She threw open the shutters and peered out at the dismal grey sky, the clouds so low they almost touched the tops of the trees, threatening more snow at any moment.

She groaned. Rosa wouldn't let her out if it snowed again, and Sara felt as if she would burst if she had to wait any longer. *I'm sixteen and I've every right to know about my family*, she thought angrily.

The morning's lessons dragged on. Sara, lost in her thoughts, only half listened to her ancient tutor droning on about political reforms. She jumped as he slammed his fist on the desk.

'Lady Sara, it is difficult enough as it is to teach you anything, but I ask you to do me the courtesy of listening to me, at least,' he said, frowning.

'I'm sorry,' she replied, putting her fountain pen down. 'It's this weather, I'm finding it hard to concentrate.'

'Hmm. We shall finish here today, tomorrow I expect you to pay more attention. I will have words with the contessa.'

Sara gathered her books, pen and inkpot, and made a hasty

retreat to her bedroom. Snow still threatened, so she would have to be quick if she were to go to the stables before her mother called for her.

She ran down to the kitchen and persuaded Rosa to give her a bag of bread and apples for the horses, then pulled on her boots and cloak and went outside. The air was heavy and cold, and everywhere was silent, waiting for the snow to cover everything in a white blanket again.

The horses whinnied when they saw her, and Bernardo poked his head over a stable door.

'Lady Sara,' he said, his smile making the wrinkles on his face even more pronounced. 'I thought you wouldn't come. How was your luncheon yesterday?'

Sara grimaced. 'You know, the usual. The duke spoke interminably about business and how well he's doing, and the duchess simpered over "how wonderful the soup is today, Lucrezia. You must tell me your cook's secret!"' She mimicked the duchess's high-pitched voice to perfection, and Bernardo burst out laughing.

'At least it's over now. Come in here, we can talk while I'm grooming Maia.'

'Just a minute.' Sara shook the bag, and Bernardo nodded in understanding.

'They'll think it's Christmas all over again,' he remarked and disappeared back inside the stable.

Sara went from stall to stall, feeding each horse until her bag was empty. She rolled it up and tucked it in her cape pocket, then went to where Bernardo was brushing a bay mare, its coat gleaming.

'I guessed you would come back today, even if there was ten metres of snow,' he said with a grin. 'Nothing stops you when you get a bee in your bonnet, right?'

Sara leaned against the stable door. 'I'd like to hear about

Nonna. She died when I was little, and I don't remember anything, and Mamma won't speak about her at all. Papà tells me not to bother her as she'll get one of her migraines and have to take to her bed, and none of the servants will tell me anything, not even Rosa. Was she a bad person, Bernardo?'

He snorted. 'Your grandmother? No, she was the finest person I ever had the good luck to meet. Your grandfather, he was different, let's say. But Lady Ginevra, she had an indomitable spirit.'

'Will you tell me about her?' Sara pleaded.

'I said I would, and I will.' Bernardo slapped the horse's withers. 'You'll do, my beauty. Let's go and sit in the harness room.'

Sara followed him to the room where saddle trees and collar brackets holding each horse's harness lined the walls, everything neatly ordered and gleaming with cleanliness. She breathed in the heady perfume of leather and oil, the aroma evoking childhood memories and a sense of peace within her. He pulled out two stools and gestured to her to sit down, then closed the door.

'Less chance of being overheard in here.' Bernardo reached over to a nearby shelf and took down a small package. 'This is for you.'

Sara turned it over in her hands. 'What is it?'

'Open it and you'll find out,' he said with a sad smile.

Her hands trembling slightly, Sara undid the string tied around it and pulled the brown paper away. She found herself gazing at a miniature portrait of her grandmother. The painting in the library had been a good likeness, but this was even more detailed. It was like looking at her reflection – the same auburn-coloured curls framed a heart-shaped face, green eyes staring in open defiance at whoever had painted the picture. She put her hand to her mouth, overcome.

'She gave that to me many years ago, and I've kept it safe ever since,' Bernardo said. 'Now it's yours.'

'I can't take this–' Sara said, but Bernardo interrupted her.

'I insist. I'm old, and I can't take it with me when I'm gone. She was your grandmother, and now you have something to remember her by.'

'Why did she give it to you?' Sara knew that a woman usually gave a man her portrait when they were– She gasped. 'W-were you...?' She hardly dared say the word. 'Lovers,' she managed to whisper in the end.

Bernardo sat back on his stool, gazing down his long nose at her. He rubbed his chin, his unshaven whiskers making a rasping sound against the rough skin of his hands.

Sara balled her hands into fists. 'I demand to know.'

'I stayed up most of the night thinking about what to tell you.'

'I want you to tell me the truth.'

Bernardo shook his head. 'Some truths are best hidden away.'

'People have been hiding things from me all my life,' Sara retorted. 'I have a right to know, don't you think?'

Bernardo gave a deep sigh. 'Let me tell you the whole story, then, so you'll understand.'

Sara nodded, dreading what she was about to hear.

'I was fifteen when I started working here at the villa, only a stable lad who kept his eyes to the ground and his nose clean. Your grandmother was a couple of years older than me and, like I told you yesterday, she taught me to love horses instead of being scared of them. She was fearless, and would go riding any time she could, always on that black stallion of hers. Zeus, he was the great-grandsire of Apollo. He was a devil, but quiet as a lamb with her. Her father was worried she'd break her neck, so old Gianni had to accompany her when she went out. One day he was ill, and he asked me to go. She was that pleased; said Gianni fussed too much and never went faster than a trot. She hated being held back, your nonna.

'Anyway, she made sure to ask for me after that, and we became good friends, always laughing and talking about something. We'd go on long hacks through the woods or up in the mountains. She pushed that stallion to its limits, and he gave her everything he had.'

Sara closed her eyes and imagined her grandmother, long auburn hair flying behind her, galloping through the mountains, the powerful black stallion's legs covering vast distances.

'She had one other passion, though, which took up the rest of her time. She was a healer.'

'Ah, yes. You mentioned that yesterday,' Sara said, opening her eyes and concentrating fully on him. 'What's that?'

'Something every Innocenti should know about, Lady Sara.' Bernardo shook his head and fell silent, his brow furrowed.

Sara waited for him to speak again, unaware that his words would change her life forever.

5

'Your poor grandmother would be turning in her grave, you not knowing what a healer is,' Bernardo said sadly, his eyes watery. 'But thanks to your grandfather – well, we'll get to that later. Your grandmother, and her mother before her, and hers before, were healers. Generations of women, from time immemorial. She lived here at the villa, but used the cottage to prepare her remedies. People would come from all over the place for her cures, and she never asked them for money. Some would give her furs, or animals they'd trapped, or eggs, which she quietly accepted every time. Said it gave them dignity.'

'What? A cottage?'

'Yes, in the woods. She inherited it from her mother and should have gone to live there when she married, but your grandfather was determined to live at the villa and wouldn't hear of them going there.'

'Grey stone walls, with a separate vegetable patch in the garden?' Sara asked, excited.

'That's the one. Only it wasn't a vegetable patch. That was where she grew all her healing plants.' He narrowed his eyes. 'How do you know about it?'

'You probably won't believe this, but a couple of months ago I was out in the snow and I saw a dragonfly. I-I felt compelled to follow it and ended up at the cottage. I wanted to go in, but the door was locked.' She stopped as the image of the woman in the kitchen appeared before her, and blinked to get rid of it. 'So I walked down the garden, found the gate, and went inside. There was a fountain too. But everything was covered in snow. I'd like to go back now the snow's gone.'

'The dragonflies,' Bernardo said.

'What?'

'The garden – the Grove, she called it – was always full of dragonflies in the spring and summer. You should have seen it, like jewels flying in the air, it was. And every time she went in there, they'd swarm around her. It was incredible. She loved that place, and it broke her heart when your grandfather forbade her to go there anymore.'

'Why did he do that?'

'Ginevra was very skilled at what she did. People who were so sick they should have died miraculously got better again, babies at death's door began sucking their mother's milk and putting on weight; and so the rumours started.

'First hereabouts, then they spread throughout the valley. Your grandmother was a witch, she was in league with the devil, she *was* the devil.'

'The people she helped make better accused her of being a witch?' Sara exclaimed.

'No, no. The villagers tried to quell the rumours. Those who were spreading them were the other landowners, the traders, anyone who held a modicum of power. They were jealous, you see – she was popular with the villagers, they'd do anything for her, and the others, they didn't like that. So one day, your grandfather told Lady Ginevra she wasn't to go to the cottage anymore. It would be closed up, and she wasn't to prepare any more remedies or help cure the locals. If she did, she'd be locked away in an institute as a mad woman, and he wouldn't be able to prevent it.' Bernardo bowed his head, his eyes avoiding hers. 'This is the part you might not like, Lady Sara, and I'm sorry. But it happened, and I can't change that.'

'Go on.'

'Your grandmother came to the stables, she was in a terrible state. She fell into my arms and started sobbing. I didn't know what to do, so I got the horses ready and we rode off into the woods. To the cottage. She took me inside and we, we...' He twisted his hands together, his cheeks bright red.

'You and Nonna!'

Bernardo reached out to her, but she batted his hand away. 'Sara, please. I loved Lady Ginevra. I loved her from the moment I set eyes on her, and she loved me, but we had to live with the knowledge that she could never be mine, no matter how much we wanted it.'

'Don't.' She couldn't bear it. The thought of her grandmother and Bernardo...

'I knew the truth would be too much for you.' The old man shook his head, tears welling up in his eyes. 'I hoped you would understand. What a fool I am.' He leaned forward, his elbows on his knees, and buried his head in his hands.

Despite her turmoil, Sara's heart ached for Bernardo. His only fault had been to fall in love with the wrong person. He must have suffered untold sorrow all these long years.

'I'm sorry,' she said. 'Please, continue. I do understand. It was a terrible shock, that's all.' She tried to relax her shoulders and neck; her jaw already ached from clenching it so tightly.

Bernardo looked up at her. 'If you're sure.'

Sara nodded.

He clasped his hands in his lap. 'Where was I? Oh, yes. Afterwards, she told me what her husband had said. She was so distraught, she couldn't bear to think of the villagers left without any help. She said that Lucrezia had seen your grandfather hit her, and heard his threats, and that upset her more than anything. The thought that there would be no more healers after her, it broke her heart.'

'Mamma was there? No wonder she doesn't want me going to the cottage.' This explained her mother's anger.

Bernardo took his handkerchief out of his pocket and wiped his forehead. 'We made a pact. I went to the cottage a couple of times a week and tended the plants, made sure everything was kept in order. She would give me a list of what she needed and I would take it back to her, up at the villa. Together with Anna-Maria, her most trusted friend, and Lucia, Rosa's mother, she made small batches of her remedies, and I took them down to the village. That way she made sure her cures reached those who needed them. It wasn't perfect, but it was better than nothing.'

'My grandfather never found out?'

Bernardo twisted the handkerchief in his hands, his head lowered. 'No. Lucia helped cover up Ginevra's activities in the kitchen. Your grandmother had promised him she would stop, and Ludovico had no reason not to believe her. No one spoke about her cures anymore, so he was satisfied he'd put an end to it.'

'And what about you and her?' Sara asked softly. Now that the initial shock had passed, she wanted to know everything.

'I loved her,' Bernardo said, finally raising his head. 'I knew what would happen to her if your grandfather found out about us, he was a violent man when he grew angry. We had that one time together, we both knew it could never happen again. Sometimes I caught her looking at me, that lost look in her eyes; the same look I'm sure I had too.' He rubbed at his eyes and sniffed. 'After she died, there was no need to keep the cottage and the Grove going. Your mother refused to learn to be a healer, she said she wouldn't go against her father's wishes. The book and the chest, they went to your mother, but I have no idea what she did with them. She might have burned them for all I know, to put an end to your family's tradition.'

'A book?'

'Lady Ginevra had a recipe book, full of remedies written by previous healers during the centuries. Every healer added her own recipes and drawings, it was invaluable to your grandmother. She kept it in a wooden chest with a dragonfly carved on the lid. By rights, it should be yours.'

'I'll search for it. Perhaps Mamma has hidden it somewhere in the house.'

'You'll only get into trouble,' Bernardo said, shaking his head. 'Best leave it, Lady Sara.'

'But the cottage!' Sara jumped to her feet, the stool skittering across the floor. 'We can't let it fall to ruins. And the Grove, the plants, we must save them. Perhaps I can learn, even without the book.'

Bernardo picked up the stool. 'Lady Sara, it must be a secret. No one can know. The servants will be watching you and they will tell the contessa. We must be careful.' His voice was low and urgent.

Sara looked at him, surprised. 'We? You'll help me?'

'If you'll let me. I know a bit about the plants, I can teach you. The rest, you will have to find out for yourself. But you mustn't talk with anyone, otherwise I'll be out on my ear and you'll be confined to the villa for the rest of your life. Understood?'

'Understood.' Sara clasped the portrait of her grandmother to her chest, her mind whirling with emotions as she tried to imagine what it would be like to be a healer.

6

Spring arrived late that year, but finally the snow melted and winter loosened its grip on the countryside. The trees were covered in green buds, and daffodils and crocuses poked their stalks through the cold earth, seeking the sun's warmth.

Sara had kept herself busy since speaking with Bernardo. Impatient to start working in the Grove, she searched the library for books on plants and absorbed all the information she could find, anything on how to care for them and use them for curing various ailments. She also looked for the book and chest Bernardo had mentioned, without any luck. She even dared to enter her mother's chambers one afternoon, having seen the carriage leave for a luncheon at their neighbours' estate. She knew she had a good few hours before they came back, so had taken her time, opening every drawer and examining every cupboard. All to no avail.

Whenever she went to the stables, she was careful not to mention the cottage or the Grove. There could be ears anywhere – a stable boy hidden in a stall, one of the maids on her way to the villa's vegetable garden, or Rosa checking up on her, as she frequently did nowadays.

'The weather's clearing up, spring is on its way,' Bernardo said to her one morning as they led two horses to the paddock. 'Snow's practically gone, the ground will be ready for planting soon.' He turned and winked at her.

'That's great news. Papà will be pleased they can start preparing the fields for the crops. He was complaining just the other day about how long this winter has been.' Sara felt adrenalin rush through her, making her tingle with excitement.

'Won't be long now, tell him.' Bernardo turned to her, his face hidden by the horse's flank. 'Are you sure you want to do this?'

Sara smiled. 'More than anything. I've been learning all about caring for the plants, I want to carry on my grandmother's work.'

'Healing's in your blood. Ginevra's greatest hope was that someone would take her place. She'll be able to rest in peace now.'

***

Sara hesitated as they approached the back door of the cottage. They had managed to slip away without being seen and had met up in the woods, making their way through the trees without saying a word. Now she was back here, she remembered the image of the ghostly figure she had seen through the window, and wondered if she would see it again.

'Are you all right?' Bernardo asked.

'I...' Sara squared her shoulders. 'Yes, let's go inside.'

Bernardo turned the handle and the door swung open with a loud creak. They went in, blinking after the bright sunlight outside. Dust motes hung in the air, and there was a musty smell. The first thing she noticed were two ornately carved armchairs, lined with what looked like red damask fabric, although there was so much dust she couldn't be sure of the original colour. A sturdy dresser lined the far wall, near the stairs, and a large wooden table divided the kitchen from the living room.

China cups hung from hooks beneath one of the kitchen cupboards, and the marble counter was scattered with mouse droppings and debris. A ceramic sink, its surface covered in tiny cracks, took up most of one wall.

Bernardo strode over to the sink and opened the window, breaking the cobwebs hanging there. A large black spider scuttled away, disappearing down a crevice in the wall.

'It'll need a bit of cleaning and fixing, but it won't take long,' he said. 'I'll check the chimney isn't blocked, you'll need the fire as well as the stove for boiling all the infusions.'

Sara stood, staring at the fireplace. She'd half-expected to see the woman there, stirring the pot, and was almost disappointed that she wasn't.

'Lady Sara?' Bernardo's tone was polite but with a hint of worry.

She forced herself to concentrate on why they were there. 'Yes, of course. It's pointless we clean anything until you've cleared the chimney, so shall I go out to the Grove?'

'I can tell you're eager to get your hands on those plants,' Bernardo said with a laugh. 'That's all right. You go and see what needs doing there, while I make a start here. Call me if you want some help with anything.'

Sara left the house, glad to get away. It no longer scared her, but she felt sad, as if a part of her history had been destroyed and there was no way for her to get it back. A wave of grief washed over her, and she wished she had known her grandmother for longer, so that she'd had time to pass her knowledge on to Sara. She was upset with her mother for turning her back on her family's traditions, and in particular for never having said anything about their past.

The wooden gate creaked as Sara opened it and went inside the Grove. A dragonfly flitted past her face, its wings almost brushing her skin, making her jerk her head back. Without its blanket of snow, at long last Sara could see the garden, and felt like weeping. Tangles of weeds covered the plants, slowly choking them, and the rows, which she imagined had once been neat and tidy, were a sprawling mass of overgrown vegetation.

'I've got lots to do here,' Sara said with a sigh. She reached into her pocket, took out the knife and scissors she'd 'borrowed' from the kitchen up at the villa, and looked about, trying to decide where to start.

She went over to the fountain and sat on its edge, leaning back with her hands on the cold marble. She jumped as she felt a tickle, then laughed when she saw the dragonfly perched on the back of her hand. It took off immediately and flew over to some bedraggled plants near one of the walls, where it landed on the tip of one and hovered there, the plant bobbing up and down in time with the beat of its wings.

'I think you want me to start with these ones.' Sara bent down and tenderly lifted the frostbitten leaves of the plant. She wondered briefly how she knew what the dragonfly wanted her to do, but soon forgot about it as she tended to the plants.

7

They couldn't get to the cottage every day, and didn't always go together, so as not to rouse suspicion. The hardest part for Sara was slipping out of the villa without any of the servants seeing her. Too often she would have to turn back as Rosa called out to her, or one of the gardeners suddenly appeared from behind a hedge he was pruning.

Her father was away on business, yet again, but her mother was usually at home, and seemed to be keeping a close eye on her. Sara seethed every time her plans to go to the cottage were thwarted, resigning herself to tedious afternoons perched on an uncomfortable chair, sewing, while her mother read or went over the estate's accounts with the steward.

When she did manage to get away, Sara usually headed straight for the Grove. The few times she went inside the cottage, she caught glimpses of a shadowy figure that disappeared as soon as she turned around. However, it no longer frightened her; she felt comforted somehow, as if her grandmother were there, watching over her. She didn't mention it to Bernardo, but she wondered if he sensed Ginevra's presence too.

Bernardo worked inside the house, clearing the chimney, repairing the window frames, and replacing any rotting wood. Once he had finished, he cleaned every room, although he left the windows.

'We don't want anyone asking why the windows are clean and shiny,' he told Sara. 'We'll leave them as they are, makes it look like the place is still abandoned. You mustn't cut the hedge around the Grove or tidy up the garden, for the same reason.'

'Why is there a driveway underneath the grass in the clearing?' Sara asked him. Since the snow had melted, she'd noticed patches of red bricks or tiles showing through the grass, and wondered what had once been there.

'There used to be a road linking the cottage to the villa. It fell into disuse when your grandmother could no longer come here, and Mother Nature has slowly taken back what was once hers.' He sighed, and Sara could see his thoughts were elsewhere, lost in the past. She stood silently beside him, saddened that the cottage held such bittersweet memories for Bernardo.

Sara enjoyed spending her time in the garden, clearing away the weeds, turning the soil around each plant, adding mulch to fertilise them. She wore an old pair of leather riding gloves whenever she could to avoid ruining her hands, knowing her mother would notice any dirt under her fingernails right away.

Slowly but surely, they made the cottage liveable once more, and the garden flourished under Sara's care. As the days grew warmer, there were more and more dragonflies, until clouds of them rose in the air every time they went into the Grove.

'You've done a great job, Lady Sara,' Bernardo said, looking around in awe as they walked among the plants and bushes. He stopped under an apple tree, loaded with delicate pink and white blossom. 'Your grandmother would be so happy to see the garden like this again.'

Sara patted his arm. 'Thank you for all your help.'

'I did it for her, as well as for you,' he said softly, his gaze fixed on some invisible spot in the far distance.

Sara sensed his grief, and knew he was thinking about all those years before. 'Nonna would be grateful for everything you've done.'

He straightened his shoulders. 'Shall we see if there's anything in the pantry and start trying out some recipes?' He wiped his hand under his nose, and Sara pretended not to see the tears at the corners of his eyes.

'I'd love to!' she exclaimed. They'd discovered the pantry while sorting out the cottage, with its shelves of glass jars filled with desiccated leaves and berries, and hoped they would find something in there they could use.

They spent a pleasant afternoon opening the jars and identifying the contents either by studying or sniffing them. Bernardo remembered some of the preparations he had helped make, and soon the cottage was full of the aroma of herbs boiling on the cast iron stove.

'Won't someone see the smoke?' Sara asked.

'If they do, I'll say I made a bonfire to burn some brambles from the paddock. Don't worry, we're deep in the woods here and nobody comes this way.'

Sara hoped he was right, but her brow remained creased in worry.

'This time it seems to be coming better than our other attempts,' Bernardo remarked, sniffing the concoction they were brewing. Their previous two tries had ended up being poured away outside, one smelling as if it had been left to rot for a couple of years, the other a thick grey sludge that no one in their right mind would even think about drinking.

'It couldn't come much worse,' Sara replied with a laugh. She leaned over and stirred the mixture. 'At least it has a nice colour. What is it for?'

Bernardo frowned. 'If I remember rightly, it helps with stomach cramps and the like.' He grimaced. 'I'll try it first, though, make sure it won't poison anyone!'

'If only we had the recipe book.' Sara sighed, frustrated. She'd searched everywhere, but still hadn't found it.

'I hope the contessa hasn't thrown it on the fire,' Bernardo said.

'She wouldn't! No matter how much she hated the healers, she wouldn't destroy such a valuable heirloom.'

'I hope you're right. I only saw it once, but it was a fine book. All bound in leather, and every page crammed with recipes and drawings. Every healer wrote their name in the front; Ginevra showed me where she'd written hers. She knew almost every recipe off by heart, so she said.'

'I'd love to see it.' Sara lifted the pot off the stove. 'Shall we bottle this up and leave it to cool, then come back tomorrow and see how it is?'

'It's getting late. You go back up to the villa now, and I'll finish off here.' Bernardo glanced out of the window. 'The contessa will be upset if you're not back in time for afternoon tea.'

'I wish...' Sara paused, a movement to her side distracting her for a moment. A soft breeze blew against her cheek, almost as if fingertips were brushing over her skin, and made her shiver.

'You wish what?' Bernardo asked, looking at her with a curious expression on his face.

Sara shook her head, trying not to show her unease. 'It's just that it's so peaceful here at the cottage, and in the Grove. Sometimes I wish I could live here instead of the villa.'

Bernardo snorted. 'Be careful what you wish for, Lady Sara. There are greater forces at work in the world, you never know who's listening.'

Sara burst out laughing. 'You say the funniest things sometimes, Bernardo. Nothing's going to happen.'

'You're sure about that, Lady Sara? I can feel your grandmother's presence here in the cottage, and I think you do, too.'

'Nonsense,' Sara retorted, but she wrapped her shawl tighter around her shoulders.

'Go home, it's getting late.' Bernardo reached over and patted her hand.

She looked down at his rough, calloused fingers, knobbly with arthritis and years of hard work with the horses, and felt guilty for having laughed at him.

'Don't stay too long, either. You've been up since before dawn, you must be exhausted.'

His eyes twinkled. 'They say there's no rest for the devil, right? Don't worry, I'll be quick. I've got a mare about to foal at any moment, so I can't dawdle either.'

'Is that Ester?'

'Yes. She was restless this morning, so I'm pretty sure it's going to happen today or tomorrow.'

Sara gave him a hug. 'Call me when it's born, I'd love to see it! Well, I'll be going, then, before Mamma sends out a search party.'

As she walked away from the cottage, she looked back and saw Bernardo through the open door. He had his back to her, and his hand was reaching towards a shadowy figure standing before him. Sara gasped and ran across the clearing into the woods, away from the ghosts in the cottage.

8

Sara pulled on her lacy white gloves, hoping they would hide the scratches and chipped fingernails she'd got from working in the Grove, even though she'd tried to protect her hands. Her mother was waiting in the drawing room downstairs, and Sara knew from experience that she'd pick on the slightest fault she could find. She tutted in frustration as she struggled with the gloves; she was still hot and bothered from the altercations she'd had with Rosa shortly before.

The servant had been waiting impatiently for her when she'd got back to the villa, tapping her foot on the ground as Sara reached the kitchen door.

'I served the tea twenty minutes ago. Your mother was expecting you to join her in the drawing room, she says this is the third time this week you've been late. What do you do all afternoon?' Standing with her feet firmly apart and her hands on her hips, Rosa was a formidable adversary and Sara hadn't had the energy to deal with her.

'Out of my way, otherwise I'll be even later, won't I?' she'd shouted.

Rosa had been so shocked, she'd moved to the side and let her enter without another word.

Now that she'd had time to calm down, Sara regretted being so harsh with Rosa, but she was terrified her mother would find out that she and Bernardo had been to the cottage. She took a deep breath to fortify herself, and slowly made her way downstairs.

'Mamma, I'm so sorry I'm late,' she gushed as she entered the drawing room. 'I was out in the grounds and lost track of time.' Her voice faded as she noticed the other person in the room. 'Papà! You're home.' She hoped they couldn't hear the disappointment in her voice.

'I had to come. Your mother sent me a telegram asking me to return immediately due to your behaviour.' He stood, tall and stiff, by the fireplace, hands clasped behind his back, his face stern as he spoke.

'My behaviour?' Sara repeated, flustered. She glanced at her mother, sat in her usual armchair.

'You're late for almost every meal, and when I send the servants to search for you, you are nowhere to be found,' Lucrezia said, her icy gaze boring into Sara. 'When I ask what you've been doing, you avoid looking at me and give me vague answers that do not justify your absences. Given your age and your secretive nature, I had no option but to ask your father to come home. I'm sure he can find out what's going on.'

'But–' How would she come up with an explanation that would satisfy her parents while not revealing what she was really doing?

'I had to break off a very important business meeting in order to return here, I'm not best pleased.' Her father's face was white with anger, his lips firmly pressed together as he studied her. Sara wondered if she should sit down on one of the sofas before her legs gave way, but one glance at her parents' faces convinced her it would be best to remain standing.

'Speak,' he barked.

Sara cleared her throat. 'I've been helping Bernardo up at the stables,' she said, thinking it was better to keep as close to the truth as possible.

'I sent Rosa up to the stables several times, she never saw you there,' her mother snapped.

'He's been teaching me about plants and animals. We go into the woods and follow tracks or stop and study any unusual plants we find.'

'Liar!'

Sara took a step backwards, shocked by the venom in her mother's voice.

'Rosa said she asked Bernardo where you were, and he told her he hadn't seen you.' Sara was relieved that he hadn't got into trouble on her account. 'Tell us the truth. Several of the servants have told us they've seen you heading towards the woods. Alone.' Her mother's chest heaved as she spoke, and Sara knew she was on the point of exploding. The contessa's temper was legendary in the house; every single one of the servants had been at the receiving end of her rants at one time or another.

'Is there a boy?' her father asked, spitting out the words.

'What?' How could they think such a thing?

'Is that why you've been sneaking off into the woods?' Lucrezia hissed. 'Who is he, someone from the village? Some peasant boy you've fallen in love with?' Her voice rose, her cheeks flushing red as her hands gripped the arms of the chair.

'No, no, it's nothing like that,' Sara insisted.

Her father stepped forward and grabbed hold of her shoulders. 'What else can it be? Why else would our daughter lie to us, why else would she disappear into the woods all alone? Why?'

Sara burst into tears, distraught they would think such a thing of her. She wriggled out of her father's grasp, desperate to escape from the room, far away from them both. She looked wildly about, searching for a way to get past her parents.

'You little whore. What next? Are you going to tell us you're carrying a bastard child, perhaps?' Her mother's sneering voice cut through the haze in Sara's head, the scathing words crushing her with their weight.

'I'm not sneaking out to see a boy,' she sobbed, tears pouring down her cheeks. Her shoulders drooped and her bottom lip trembled. 'And I promise you I'm not carrying anyone's child.'

'Hmph.' Her father crossed his arms, his eyes narrowed. Her mother sat rigid in her chair, the look on her face saying more than any words could.

Sara took a few heaving breaths. The injustice of the situation was more than she could bear. Her head roared as the blood pumped through her veins, her emotions overwhelming her. She owed it to her grandmother, and to all the healers, to tell her parents what she had really been doing.

'All right,' she shouted, surprising herself as much as her parents. The room fell silent, their eyes fixed on her. She looked down at the ground, then raised her chin defiantly and stared directly at them. 'I've been going to the cottage. To Nonna Ginevra's cottage.'

Her mother slowly got up out of her chair and stood before Sara. Her hand landed on Sara's cheek with a loud crack. Sara cried out in pain, clasping her palm against her throbbing cheek, and cowered away from her mother.

'You stupid girl,' Lucrezia shrieked. 'You stupid, stupid girl. How many times have I told you not to go into the woods? I've done everything I can to keep you away from there, but still you disobey me, still you go behind my back! The cottage is bad luck, nothing good ever comes from that place. So many people have died there. The very ground it stands on is cursed.' She sank back into her chair, fanning herself with her hand. 'Why did you go, anyway? It's a dirty, run-down old cottage, nothing special.'

'I found the Grove,' Sara replied, still not looking at her mother. The throbbing in her cheek was reduced to a dull ache, but she knew she would never forgive her.

'The Grove? How did you find it?' Her mother frowned. 'And how did you know it was called the Grove?'

'A dragonfly led me there.'

Lucrezia snorted. 'Again that ridiculous story! We're supposed to believe a dragonfly took you to the cottage. And it spoke to you and told you about the Grove, did it?'

'No, Bernardo told me about–' Sara stopped as she realised what she'd done.

'*Bernardo*! I knew I should have sent him away when my mother died.' Lucrezia leaned forward, pointing a long, bony finger at Sara. 'You are never to go back there, do you hear me? I'll have the cottage torn down and the Grove destroyed.'

'No!' Sara yelled. 'No, you can't, not the plants or the cottage! I want to carry on my grandmother's work, become a healer.'

Her father grabbed hold of her arm and dragged her across the floor. 'Haven't you been listening to a word your mother said?' he shouted. 'You... are... not... to... go... back.' At every word he cuffed her around the head, until her ears were ringing and the room spun around her. When he let go of her she dropped to the ground in a heap, her arms splayed as she tried to stop the world turning.

'I hate you!' Sara shouted, the words muffled inside her head by the ringing in her ears. 'I hate you both. Why don't you want me to carry on Nonna's work? Why didn't *you* become a healer?' She glared at her mother.

Lucrezia sank back into her armchair, her face white and pinched. 'Do you really want to know why?'

Sara dreaded what her mother would say. 'Yes,' she whispered, her head hung low.

'Your nonna became the talk of the area. The villagers may have loved her, but the landowners called her a troublemaker, and worse. Rumours spread of her being a witch, that her remedies were unnaturally potent, that not even the best doctors in the country were able to cure as many ailments as she could. Your grandfather forbade her to carry on, in part to protect the reputation of the family, but also to prevent her being exorcised by the priest or locked up in a mental asylum.' Her face twisted into a grimace as she spoke.

'I was there when he told her to stop. It was in this very room, in fact. I was hiding behind that sofa over there. He didn't know I was here, but she did. After he beat her she looked over at me, and I saw it in her eyes – he could beat her every day for the rest of her life but she wasn't going to stop, she would merely find another way to make her potions. I vowed then and there that it would end with her, that there would be no more healers, no more gossip, no more death in this family.'

'No one can be shut up in a mental asylum for no reason, that's ridiculous,' Sara said. 'I don't believe you, there's some other reason why you don't want me to become a healer.'

Her father clenched his fist and took a step towards her, but Lucrezia held out her hand to stop him.

'People are locked up for lesser reasons than that, my naïve daughter. Being accused of witchcraft would be a life sentence in an institution nowadays, but back in your grandmother's time, it would have meant torture and perhaps death if she wouldn't renounce her ways. It was a serious accusation.' She brought her hand to her forehead and sighed wearily. 'My mother told me this day would come. In her last weeks, she talked incessantly about the healers and how important it was to carry on the tradition. She said...' Lucrezia stopped, frowning as she tried to remember. 'She said that healing was in our blood, and no matter how much I denied it, it would come out sooner or later. It was our calling, our inevitable *need* to tend the Grove and cure people afflicted by disease. If not me, then you. She doted on you, you know.'

Sara waited, hardly daring to breathe. The three of them seemed suspended in an artist's oil painting: her, on the floor, skirts spread around her, clasping her hands to her chest in supplication to her parents; her father, standing tall and proud over her, his hands ready to lash out and strike; her mother, white skin harsh against her black dress, sat upright in her armchair as though bestowing judgement on her daughter.

'You can beat her to within an inch of her life, but Sara is as stubborn as my mother was,' Lucrezia said to her husband. 'And destroying the cottage and the Grove won't solve anything, she'll find a way to do it anyway. I knew this day would come.' She turned to Sara, a grim smile on her face. 'The best way to punish you for your insolence is to send you away.'

'Send me away?' Sara had been sure her mother was going to give in. Where would she send her? She would fight any decision to the bitter end.

'Where do you have in mind?' Her father looked down at Lucrezia, frowning.

'To the cottage.' Lucrezia sat back, a satisfied smile on her face.

'The cottage?' Sara was confused.

'Yes. You love the place so much, go and live there. Without any servants, of course. It will be interesting to see how long it takes you to come crawling back and apologise. I give you a week. And Bernardo will have to go too. I can't bear to even look at him after this.'

Her father cleared his throat. 'The locals say the cottage is haunted, but that won't bother you, after all the time you've been spending there lately,' he said in a pompous tone. 'And, young lady, I would advise you don't come crawling back here, because next time your mother won't be able to stop me from giving you the beating you deserve. For now, I would say that this punishment is adequate.'

Sara put her hands over her face and wept, aware of her parents watching her dispassionately. But while her heart was breaking over the way they could discard her like that, tossing her aside as if she'd never mattered to them, her mind was already racing ahead. The thought of sleeping at the cottage, in the dark, alone except for her grandmother's ghost, filled her with unease. She pushed the misgivings from her mind. The cottage was hers, and she could become a healer. That would suffice for now, although she felt deeply sorry for Bernardo being sent away. She knew he would miss his horses. Fresh tears burst forth as she realised her life was about to change, and she had no idea which direction it would take.

'Stop your snivelling,' her mother snapped, rising out of her chair. 'Go upstairs and pack your things, I want you out of this house by nightfall.'

Her cold, harsh tone cut Sara to the quick. She wiped her eyes, a flash of rebellion rushing through her. She gathered her skirts and staggered to her feet. 'What will you tell the neighbours, Mamma? How will you explain your only daughter living in that old, run-down cottage? What about your *bella figura*?'

Her mother glared at her, her eyes dark with anger. 'I will tell everyone you've gone mad, just like your grandmother and her mother before her,' she said coldly. 'Don't worry, by the time I've finished everyone will be "oh, so understanding".' Her voice dripped with sugary sweetness.

'Thank you, Mamma, it's a pleasure to know that your social upstanding won't suffer due to my stubbornness.' Sara brushed some dust from her skirts, then turned and walked out of the room, leaving her parents in shocked silence behind her.

9

Sara went up to her room and sat on her bed, stunned. The afternoon's events had escalated far beyond anything she could have imagined. Her cheek still stung where her mother had slapped her, and she had dark spots at the edge of her vision, presumably caused by her father's blows to her head. She looked around, hardly believing this was the last time she would see the room she'd grown up in, filled with treasured objects from her childhood.

She picked up a horse carved from wood many years before by Bernardo, its mane billowing as it reared up on its hind legs, and turned it in her hands, the wood dark and smooth after all the hours she'd spent playing with it. On a shelf above her bed were the glass trinkets her father had brought back from his many trips to Venice. She could still remember falling asleep as he recounted his time on the tiny island of Murano in the Venetian Lagoon, famous for its glassmaking, watching the artisans blow the glass into a myriad of wonderful, colourful shapes.

Sara started to make a mental list of the things she would take with her, an emptiness filling her soul as she realised she would have to leave most of it behind. She ran her fingertips over her beloved books, which she had read many times since she was little, and faltered. Could she really leave everything behind to become a healer?

There was a knock at the door, and Rosa entered. 'The contessa asked me to bring you this,' she said, her cheeks flushing. She handed Sara an old flour sack. 'She said this should suffice to carry your things.'

Sara took the bag. 'You know?' Somehow, the thought of her nursemaid knowing the reason why she had to leave the villa hurt more than anything else.

'Your mother told me some of it, yes. I can't decide whether you're very stupid or very brave, to tell you the truth.' She turned and looked into the hallway behind her before continuing in a low voice. 'My mother helped Lady Ginevra when she needed her most, and never betrayed her. I've looked after you since the day you were born, you're like the daughter I never had. I've always known you were different – more like your grandmother, God rest her soul, than your mother. I want you to know that you can come to me if you need anything. I won't leave you to fend for yourself because the contessa has disowned you.'

Sara took a long look at Rosa, at her kind face and rosy cheeks, her plump figure clad in the plain brown dress and white apron she always wore, long sleeves hiding surprisingly strong arms that had held her close so many times she'd lost count, and felt as if she would burst into tears.

'Thank you, Rosa, that means a lot to me. But won't you get into trouble?'

'Don't let your mother catch you, that's all, otherwise I'll be sent away too.' She turned to leave, then stopped. 'By the way, Bernardo will be looking for somewhere to live, and that cottage is more than big enough for two people.' She winked at Sara, then left the room, closing the door quietly behind her.

That was a surprise, Sara mused. She'd always thought of Rosa as her mother's tell-tale; instead, here she was, offering to help her. She picked up the cloth sack Rosa had given her and started putting her things inside it. She stuffed a couple of plain dresses, made of hard-wearing cloth that would last a while, some underwear, her thick woollen stockings she used for riding in the colder months, and some shawls and scarves into the sack, pushing them down so she could fit as much as possible in there. She added some toiletries, her hairbrush, and a couple of books, and the sack was full.

She went over to her dressing table, opened her jewellery box, and looked wistfully at the sparkling trinkets, wondering if she would ever wear them again. A thought occurred to her: if she was to be disowned by her family, she could sell some of her jewellery if necessary. At least she and Bernardo wouldn't die of starvation. She quickly tipped the jewels into the sack, cramming them down the sides and in among her clothes, desperately hoping no one would check to see what she was taking with her.

This is my inheritance! Anger made her cheeks flush red. She looked at her reflection in the mirror above the dressing table, hardly recognising herself. It was as if she'd aged ten years that afternoon. The determined expression on her face scared her for a moment, until she realised that her parents had given her no choice – she could either fight back against the injustice of the situation and prove to them that she could survive on her own, or collapse in a heap and beg them to forgive her and take her back.

Sara gave a wry smile to her reflection. 'An Innocenti never begs,' she said out loud. She clutched the sack to her chest and left her room for the last time.

The shadows of the trees stretched across the clearing as she approached the cottage. She stopped at the edge, suddenly apprehensive. Anyone could be stood behind the windows, watching her, the dirt and grime on the glass hiding them from view. Or any*thing*. The thought of ghosts no longer frightened her, but the gloomy shades of dusk made her imagination run riot. Spending the night alone in the cottage wasn't as appealing as she'd thought.

A dragonfly flitted out in front of her – *the* dragonfly, she told herself – its brightly coloured body glinting in the late-afternoon rays of the sun. Almost without realising, she held out her hand to it, her palm turned upwards in a gesture of... what? Supplication? She concentrated on the insect before her, the trees, the clearing, and the cottage fading into a grey nothingness as a brilliant yellow light shone out all around the dragonfly. She gazed deeply into its round black eyes, sensing that the creature wanted to communicate with her in some way.

Confused images flooded her mind: a cloud of dragonflies rising into the sky; people walking across rocky terrain, windswept deserts, verdant valleys, and snow-capped mountains; the dragonflies hovering in the air, the people sat on the ground below them, cross-legged, a rapturous look on each of their faces; the people setting off on their journeys back home, many to heal, some to harm. Sara's eyes opened wide with the wonder of everything she saw, her mind clearing as she understood her past, and her future.

The scenes slowly faded, the light dimming to a pulsating glow as the dragonfly finished telling her its story. It lifted up off her hand, its legs tickling her palm as it moved, and hovered before her.

'Thank you,' she whispered. All doubt gone, Sara Innocenti, the healer, strode across the clearing to the cottage, opened the door and stepped inside.

'I thought you'd never get here.' Bernardo sat at the kitchen table, smiling at her.

Sara clasped her hands to her chest. 'You made me jump!' She rushed over and hugged him, ignoring his embarrassed grimace. 'I went to the stables, but you'd already gone.'

'The servant the contessa sent made it clear I was to leave immediately if I wanted to avoid a beating, or worse. The only place I could think of going was here. If you'll let me stay.'

'Of course you can.' Sara had never been so relieved to see anyone. 'Rosa suggested I ask you to move in here, she said there was more than enough space for two.'

Bernardo chuckled. 'Rosa always had a sensible head on her shoulders. So, Lady Sara, what happens next?'

'First, you stop calling me Lady Sara. Sara will do, seeing as my parents have decided to disown me.'

'That'll take some getting used to.' He rubbed his finger over a scratch in the surface of the table.

'Second, we learn every remedy we can and start helping the locals in the village and the valley, just like my grandmother did. I want to become a healer.'

'Without the recipe book, we'll be like two blind people trying to drive a carriage.'

'We're going to have to work hard and do what we can, we'll learn as we go along. Tomorrow I'll go down to the village and speak with the women there, I'm sure someone will be able to help us.'

Bernardo looked impressed. 'It sounds like you have been thinking long about this, La–, I mean, Sara. It's a good job I started that vegetable patch in the garden, that'll keep us fed for a while. Maybe I'll get some chickens as well.'

'We can do this, can't we?' Sara sat down next to him, her legs suddenly too tired to hold her up any longer. The stress of the day's events washed over her, draining her of energy.

'I warned you to be careful what you wished for. It'll be hard for you, but I don't see any reason why not.' He reached over and held her hand. 'It's been a long day, Lady Sara. I've got some bread and cheese here – what say you we have a bite to eat then get some rest? Everything will seem easier in the morning.'

Sara was too tired to correct his use of Lady. 'I think it's a wonderful idea.' She cut herself a chunk of cheese and broke off a piece of bread. 'This tastes so good.'

'Even the simplest fare seems a feast at times like these.' Bernardo helped himself as well, and the two ate in silence.

Sara slept fitfully that night, her dreams disturbed by unsettling images she couldn't remember when she woke. A couple of times she could have sworn there was a shadowy figure standing in the corner of her bedroom, but her sleep-filled eyes closed before she could get a good look at it. She was glad when dawn finally broke and the sound of birds chirping told her it was time to get up.

Bernardo was already in the kitchen, lighting the stove in preparation for the day ahead. He put a last log on the flames and stood up, wincing as he turned to her. 'I get twinges in my back in the mornings. Give it an hour or so and it'll pass. How did you sleep?'

'Not well,' Sara admitted. 'I kept having nightmares.'

'Only to be expected, after everything that happened yesterday.' He picked up a pot full of water and grunted in pain.

'I'll do it!' Sara took the pot from him, her arms sagging from the weight, and set it on the stove. 'The first thing I need to do is find a recipe for aches and pains,' she said, watching as he sat down with a grimace.

'This is nothing, it's only an old injury. Every now and then it plays up.' He rubbed his back. 'Fell off a horse while jumping a fallen tree, doctors said I was lucky to walk again. Happened about ten years ago, and I haven't been right since. It'll probably rain later on, I'm usually good at predicting damp weather!'

'You let me know when it's giving you problems and I'll do all the lifting and carrying. Otherwise you might do yourself a mischief, and then where will we be?'

'Lady Sar–'

'I told you, I no longer go by that title. Now I'm only plain Sara, and I will do my share of the work around the cottage.'

'Yes, ma'am.' Bernardo sighed, but she could see his eyes twinkling with suppressed mirth.

She put her hands on her hips. 'And while we're here, I insist you teach me everything you know, about the plants, the garden, fixing things around the house. Before…'

'You can say it. Before I snuff it.'

'No, I didn't mean that! I meant, in case you're incapacitated in any way, not actually–' She stopped when he laughed, and snorted in frustration.

Bernardo held his hands up. 'I'm sorry, these aren't things to joke about.' He straightened his face. 'You're right, though, Sara. Best you know how to do things by yourself, just in case.'

She turned her back on him and busied herself preparing two cups for their morning coffee. She set the percolator on the stove, trying not to let him see how much his words had affected her. It occurred to her for the first time exactly how much her life had changed in the space of a few hours; there were no more servants running around after her, making sure she had everything she needed, and no doctors she could summon if either she or Bernardo got sick. She wouldn't even have had a place to stay if her parents hadn't thought it would be a terrible punishment for her. If they'd even had an inkling that she regarded it as a safe haven, they would have thrown her out with nowhere to go. She supposed she should be grateful for small mercies.

The gentle bubbling from the percolator brought her back to the present. She grabbed a cloth and wrapped it around the handle before pouring the coffee into the cups.

'In the cupboard over there, you'll find a couple of slices of Rosa's *torta della nonna*,' Bernardo said.

She found the cake, put it on a tray with the coffee, and carried everything over to the kitchen table. 'There's no sugar, I'm afraid.'

'We'll make do.' He picked up a slice of cake and took a bite, the cream filling oozing over his fingers. 'Heaven.'

She smiled and picked up the other slice. 'This is really good,' she said, spraying some crumbs on the table. She giggled, and put her hand in front of her mouth. 'Sorry.'

'Don't worry about manners here, Sara. I'll soon make sure you become one of us "ordinary" folk.'

'I see it didn't take you long to stop calling me Lady Sara,' she replied primly. 'Thank goodness!'

Bernardo snorted. 'You remind me of your grandmother, she had a fine sense of humour.' A sad look came over his face. 'I keep thinking I see her,' he whispered.

Sara jerked her head up. 'What?'

'Whenever I'm in the house, I see a shadow. It doesn't do anything, it's just there. I find it...' He paused.

'Reassuring,' Sara finished for him.

'Yes.' He glanced at her. 'You've seen it too?'

'I-I think so. I thought it was only me, but if you're seeing it, then I guess there's something here. At first it worried me, but now I find it comforting. It's as if she's keeping an eye on us.'

He leaned back in his chair, his hands clasped before him on the table. A few crumbs were all that remained of the cake. 'All this talking isn't going to get anything done,' he said brightly. 'You're going down to the village today?'

'I'd like to see if I can find someone who could help us with the remedies,' Sara replied, glad he'd changed the subject.

'I've been thinking. You should pay a visit to old Anna-Maria, widow of Giovanni the blacksmith. I've no idea where she lives or even if she's still alive, but I know she was a good friend of your grandmother's and often helped her.'

'Good idea. I'll ask down at the village where I can find her.' Sara got up and cleared away the breakfast things, rinsing the cups and plates in the bowl of water. 'Now don't you go doing too much today, rest that back of yours,' she said, drying her hands.

'Yes, Lady Sara,' Bernardo said meekly.

Sara tossed the cloth at him, laughing.

10

The sky was overcast as Sara walked down to the village, and she wondered if Bernardo's prediction of rain would come true. The rough dirt track was dry and dusty, but she knew it would become a fast-flowing torrent if it rained for long enough. She hurried down the track, and soon reached Gallicano.

She stopped at several shops to make some purchases, then slipped into the tavern on the main square to ask the whereabouts of the blacksmith's widow. She'd only been to the village on the rare occasion before, but imagined that the tavern would be the best place to inquire.

'Lady Sara, such a pleasure to see you, we haven't seen you around the village for a while,' the innkeeper's wife said. 'I always hoped you would drop in to our humble establishment one day.'

Sara felt a hint of irritation at the use of her title, but bit back her words. She didn't have time to explain. 'I'm looking for Anna-Maria, the blacksmith's wife. If she's still alive, that is.'

The woman stopped sweeping the floor and peered up at Sara. 'Old Annie? Yes, she's still with us, God bless her soul.

She's a bit out of it now, you know.' She tapped the side of her head. 'But on a good day, she has some tales to tell to anyone who'll listen. Especially about your grandmother!' She giggled loudly. Sara shifted her basket into her other hand and smiled politely. 'She was a wonderful woman, Lady Ginevra, not like… well, let's not talk about that right now.' She shook her head and made a face.

'About what?' Sara asked.

'People aren't very happy with your parents at the moment.' She looked as if she wanted to say more, but was unsure whether to continue. Sara opened her mouth to speak, but the woman interrupted her.

'I'm sure it'll all blow over soon, nothing to worry about,' she said hastily. 'Now, you need to take the south road out of the village and you'll find her cottage just beyond the old Hanging Tree. Nasty place to live, but she says she takes care of the souls of them poor wretches who had the misfortune to die there.' She made the sign of the cross on her chest. 'Personally, I would never be able to sleep easy in a place like that, but each to their own, I suppose.'

'Thank you.' Sara realised the woman wouldn't elaborate on what her parents had done to upset the villagers, and thought she would ask Bernardo. She pulled her shawl around her and turned to go.

'Would you like a drink or something, seeing as you're here?' The woman looked at her eagerly, and Sara knew the whole village would soon hear that the contessa's daughter had visited her tavern.

Sara shrugged apologetically. 'It looks like it's going to start raining at any moment, and I still have much to do. The next time I'm here, though, I'd love to stop and chat.'

The woman's face was crestfallen, but she brightened at

Sara's last words. 'I'll hold you to that,' she said. 'A bit of gossip makes my day.'

'I can imagine,' Sara said under her breath. She smiled at the innkeeper's wife. 'Thank you for your help and have a good day.'

'Come and visit again, ask for Dorotea if I'm not around.'

The woman followed her to the door, chattering incessantly. Sara breathed a sigh of relief as the door closed behind her, muffling the sound of the woman's voice. She settled her basket more comfortably on her arm and made her way to the south road.

The Hanging Tree was legendary in the area. It was an old, twisted oak with a branch sticking out at the right height, which had been used for centuries to mete out justice on criminals and innocents alike. Others had taken their own lives there, the burden of love or guilt too great for them to bear any longer. Sara shuddered as she rounded a curve and it came into sight, its deformed shape silhouetted against the grey sky. Its branches were almost bare of leaves, the tree too old to obey the will of the seasons; or perhaps it had given up after witnessing so much death and despair, she thought with a shiver.

The wind picked up as she neared it, the faint whistling sounding like the desperate cries of condemned men. The branches shook gently, and she noticed a raven sat near the top, its beady eyes watching her as she passed. She made the sign of the cross, averting her gaze in case she should see rotting carcasses swinging to and fro in the breeze.

The ramshackle cottage was indeed 'just beyond' the Hanging Tree; it was so close that the tree's outermost branches tapped against its stony wall. As Sara approached, the door creaked open and a tiny woman with wild silver hair, sapphire-blue eyes, and a wrinkled face popped her head outside. Sara hesitated, unsure of the welcome she'd receive.

'Come on in, then,' the woman said in a soft voice. Sara had been half expecting a croak and a cackle. 'The wind's chilly, the cold goes straight to my bones these days.'

Sara stepped through the door into a surprisingly cheery room. A fire crackled brightly in the grate, its warmth spreading throughout the cottage. There was only a single large room, divided into different areas, with a pallet bed in one corner, covered with a thick, luxurious quilt, and a small table and two chairs in another. An ancient-looking armchair sat in front of the fireplace, the fabric worn in places and the stuffing coming out.

The woman shuffled over to the table and gestured to Sara to sit down.

'Are you Anna-Maria?' Sara asked, putting her basket on the floor. A cat rushed over and sniffed the contents, purring loudly.

'Oh, shoo, there's nothing there for you.' The old woman flapped her hands, and the cat slinked away. She looked up at Sara, a kind expression on her face. 'Yes, I'm Anna-Maria. You've grown, Lady Sara.'

'You know who I am?'

Anna-Marie chuckled. 'Everyone knows the Innocenti round here.'

'I suppose so. I was told you knew my grandmother well.'

'Ah, dear Ginevra. We were close friends, once. She was a wonderful woman.'

'I don't remember her very well, she died when I was little. Mamma's never spoken much about her. I-I was wondering if you could tell me a bit about her.'

'You came all the way here to talk to me about your grandmother?'

'Yes. And to ask about her work as a healer. You see, I want to carry on the tradition, but Mamma won't give me the recipe book.' Sara decided not to mention her parents had thrown her out of the house, not yet.

'Your mother knows you want to become a healer?' Anna-Maria's tone was suddenly sharp.

'Of course.' Sara averted her eyes, unable to look at the old woman.

Anna-Maria reached over and took hold of her hand. 'Lady Sara, I'm willing to help you but you mustn't lie to me. Now, tell me the truth. Does your mother know?'

Sara sighed. 'Yes, but she's not happy about it.'

'That's better. Now, tell me everything.'

'I found the cottage by accident, when I followed the dragonfly into the woods.'

'A dragonfly, you say,' Anna-Maria interrupted.

Sara nodded. 'It was winter, with snow on the ground, and I thought it was unusual, so I followed it. It led me to the cottage and the Grove. Then Bernardo offered to help me fix the cottage and look after the plants, and we've spent the last couple of months doing that.'

'Bernardo!'

'Yes. He told me about my grandmother, what happened between them.'

'Did he now?'

Sara was puzzled by the old woman's tone, but carried on speaking. 'We'd sneak off to the cottage whenever we could and worked hard to put it right. But then...' Her voice faltered. 'Mamma found out. Yesterday, when I arrived back at the villa, she and my father were waiting for me. She hit me.' She touched her cheek, still feeling the sting of the slap. 'Papà hit me too, and wanted to give me a beating.'

'But you defied them.'

'Yes. She screamed at me, told me the cottage was cursed, that people had died there. But I told her I didn't care, I want to be a healer.' Her emotions threatened to overcome her as she spoke, and she took a deep breath. 'In the end, they sent me away to live in the cottage alone, with no servants and no help. Bernardo is there with me, he was told to leave as well. I want to carry on my grandmother's work, become a healer and help the people in the village and the valley, but I don't know where to start. Bernardo said you might know some of the recipes, as you used to help her.'

Anna-Maria stood, pulling her shawl around her. 'I will help you. But first, let us make a warm drink to keep the cold from our bones.'

Sara bit her lip, frustrated at having to wait, but a shiver of excitement ran through her at the thought of what the future would hold.

11

Anna-Maria finished her tea and put down her cup. Sara looked up from stroking the cat by her feet.

'That's better. Now, what were we talking about?' The old woman sat back in her chair and patted her knee, smiling when the cat jumped on her lap and purred loudly.

'My grandmother's book.' Sara sat up straight, her hands clasped together. 'Bernardo thinks you may remember some of the recipes.'

'I know some, yes.'

'Will you teach me?'

'Without the recipe book, it will be difficult. I am old now, and my memory isn't what it was. But yes, I will teach you the little I know.' She leaned forward and peered at Sara. 'Are you sure you want this? Your mother was right about the cottage being cursed. Bad things have happened there throughout the centuries.'

Sara felt goosebumps forming on her arms. 'I'm prepared for anything that may happen,' she said, with more determination than she felt.

Anna-Maria smiled. 'I'm sure your grandmother will look after you.'

'You mean her ghost? Do you really think they exist?'

'Ghost, spirit, shadow... there are many names for them. If you are a true healer, you will learn to talk to them.' She looked weary all of a sudden. 'I hear them all the time, the souls of those who have perished on the tree. Day and night they whisper to me, telling me their deepest, darkest secrets. That is my burden to bear, to bring relief to these tortured beings and send them on their way. The branches tap, and I obey their summons.' She cocked her head to one side, as if listening to some unheard voice.

Sara coughed, startling the old woman out of her trance.

'Ah, you are young and have no experience of life, child. You'll learn there are greater things in this world than what you see around you.'

Sara thought of the dragonfly and the shadowy figure she kept seeing, and nodded. 'I believe you.'

'That's always a good start,' Anna-Maria replied with a chuckle. 'Shall we begin?'

'Now?'

'No time like the present. You're here, and my mind is clear today.' She took a heavy woollen cloak off a hook near the fireplace and wrapped it around her. 'I feel the cold every moment of the day, one of the trials of getting old.'

Sara wondered how old she was, but didn't have the courage to ask. She followed Anna-Maria out into the vegetable patch at the back of the cottage.

'I'm seventy-six.' The old woman's voice startled her.

'That's a wonderful age to be.'

Anna-Maria turned to face her. 'It has its good points. I've yet to find them, but so I'm told.' She winked. 'Now, have a look here and tell me which plant is which.'

The vegetable patch wasn't as neat and tidy as the Grove, but Sara had no problem identifying the various herbs and fruit bushes. She'd learned a lot over the last few months with Bernardo, and was delighted to be able to show off her knowledge. Anna-Maria grunted every now and then, but made no comment.

'Except that one, I've no idea what it is,' Sara said, pointing at a tiny plant. 'We've got some at the Grove, only bigger, but even Bernardo doesn't know what it's called.'

Anna-Maria bent down and caressed the plant's leaves. 'Your grandmother gave me this cutting. It only seems to flourish up at your cottage, it hardly grows here. I have to use it sparingly. Ginevra called it "silver leaf", on account of its leaves, see. She didn't know much about it either, but she told me it's an important part of every recipe in the book.' She shivered as the wind picked up, and wrapped her cloak more tightly around her. 'Storm's on the way. Come, we'll take a leaf and pick some other herbs, then I'll show you what to do with them.'

Sara watched, fascinated, as Anna-Maria said a few words before picking the leaf from the plant. 'What was that?'

'You must always ask the plant permission before you take any part of it, and thank it afterwards,' Anna-Maria explained. 'That way, the plant won't suffer.'

'Really?' Sara paused. 'Will you teach it to me?'

'I thought you'd never ask! Come, you can do the next one.'

They made it indoors as the first large drops of rain began to fall, hitting the dry ground with dull thuds. Sara put the basket of herbs on the table and shook some water from her hair.

'You'd better go now, before it really starts,' Anna-Maria said, standing by the open door. 'If you hurry, you should make it back in time. It will hold off a while longer, before it really pours.'

'You're right.' Sara grabbed her shawl and put it around her shoulders. 'What about the herbs we picked?'

'They'll be fine until tomorrow. Come back in the morning.'

Sara got the impression the old woman wanted her gone. She gathered her basket and prayed the few things she'd bought earlier wouldn't get ruined by the rain.

'I'll be here tomorrow morning,' she promised, giving Anna-Maria a quick kiss on the cheek.

'Yes, of course. Now hurry, you don't want to be outside when the thunderstorm hits.' She half-pushed, half-guided Sara from the cottage, mumbling her farewells. When Sara got to the curve in the road she turned around to wave, and saw the old woman standing beneath the Hanging Tree, looking up into its branches. Sara clasped her basket more tightly and hurried on her way.

Bernardo was already indoors, looking anxiously out of the window as she burst through the door. The heavens had opened as Sara reached the clearing, and she'd had to sprint to the cottage. She put the basket on the dresser and took off her shawl, hanging it near the fire so it would dry.

'You've been gone such a long time, I wondered if you were coming back,' Bernardo said grumpily, handing her a towel.

Sara sat down on a chair, rubbing the towel over her head. 'How's your back?'

'It'll be better once the storm passes,' he grumbled.

'I hope you took it easy today.' She wiped her face and put the towel on the table.

'I've been sat in here all this time. Did you find her?'

'Yes. She lives by the Hanging Tree.'

'Really? I've heard there's a crazy old crone who lives down there and talks to ghosts,' Bernardo said, laughing.

Sara frowned at him. 'That's her. Anna-Maria.'

He stopped laughing. 'Oh. And how did you, er, get on?'

'She was a little strange to begin with,' Sara admitted. 'But she remembered my grandmother and promised to teach me some recipes. Then it started raining, and she bundled me out of her house as quickly as possible! She told me to hurry back before I got soaking wet. She was right, of course, but...' Sara could still see Anna-Maria standing under the Hanging Tree, gazing upwards, in her mind.

'I would imagine living in that place would drive anyone crazy,' Bernardo said.

'Yes, I suppose so. She told me to go back tomorrow, and we'll do something with the herbs we picked. She taught me a prayer to say every time we take something from the plants, so they don't suffer.'

Bernardo raised his eyebrows.

'I know, it sounds silly, but it can't do any harm, can it? And if I'm to become a healer, I must learn their ways. She also told me about the plant, the one you didn't know anything about.'

Bernardo sat in silence, puffing on his pipe, as Sara recounted what she'd learned that day. He harrumphed when she told him how Anna-Maria tended the souls of those who died on the tree, but she carried on regardless, eager to tell him everything.

'I want to go there every morning, so I can learn as much as possible. Even without my grandmother's book, we should be able to help the villagers. And now we know about the silver leaf, our remedies will be even more effective!'

Bernardo put his pipe on the table and leaned back in his chair. 'Be careful, Sara. Your grandmother spoke highly of Anna-Maria, but then they had a falling out and never spoke again. And down at the village they say she's mad. Maybe too much silver leaf has addled her brain! Learn from her, but we really need to get the recipe book from your mother, any way we can.'

12

Sara opened the door and looked out, a cool breeze blowing her hair around her face. The brilliant blue sky was filled with white clouds scudding overhead. Everywhere glistened, as if nature had washed the countryside, sparkling drops of water dangling from the leaves before they dripped to the ground.

Bernardo joined her on the doorstep and handed her a cup of tea made with herbs from the Grove and sweetened with honey. They stood in silence, overawed by the beauty around them.

'Wear your boots and old clothes, the roads will be awash with mud.'

'Thanks. Ever the practical one, eh?' Sara sipped her tea, breathing in the fresh spring air.

'And remember what I said. We'll try any recipe she teaches you on ourselves first. We don't want to be poisoning half the village now, do we?'

'I trust her.' Sara pointed at a dragonfly flitting through the garden. 'That must be a good omen, don't you think?'

Bernardo grunted and went back indoors. Sara remained

where she was, enjoying the peaceful chirping of the birds in the trees.

The door to Anna-Maria's cottage stood wide open, the breeze stirring up the dust on the floor.

'Hello?' Sara poked her head inside, but the cottage was empty. She went around to the vegetable patch at the back, where they'd picked the herbs the day before. Relieved, she saw the old woman bent over, digging up a patch of ground with a rusty shovel.

'Good morning,' she called.

Anna-Maria stood up with a start, putting her hand to her back. 'Ooh, you scared me,' she said, wincing. She leaned forward on her shovel and peered at Sara. 'You're the girl who came to visit me yesterday.'

'Yes. Sara.' Anna-Maria stared at her, a frown on her face. Sara tried again. 'Ginevra's granddaughter, remember? You said you'd teach me some of her remedies. I had to leave early yesterday, before the storm hit.'

'Ah, the storm.' Anna-Maria's gaze drifted to the distance. 'It was a bad one, there were lots of souls tossed about by the wind. I had to help them, otherwise they would have been lost forever, screaming their despair all the night long.'

Sara went over to her, worried. The old woman looked haggard in the early morning sun, her wrinkles more pronounced than ever.

'Let's get you inside and I'll make you a hot drink,' she said softly.

Anna-Maria gestured to the hole she'd been digging. 'I must finish this, it's for them.'

'Later. First a drink and something to eat.'

Sara took hold of the old woman's arm and gently led her back to the cottage. She sat her down in her armchair, then placed a pot of water on the wood-burning stove to boil.

'Did you get much sleep last night?' She went back to the old woman and perched on a wooden stool by the fireplace. The cold embers told her that Anna-Maria hadn't lit the fire the previous day.

'I told you, I had to watch over those souls, child,' she said crossly. 'The tree taps, and I obey.'

'It's only the branches in the wind. I can ask Bernardo to cut them back so they're not as close to the house.'

Anna-Maria snorted. 'What do you know? Fifty years I've been living here, fifty years with the souls crying out to me from the Hanging Tree. My mother lived here before me, and her mother before her, tending to the souls that called to them in the heart of the night. Giovanni understood. He was the only one. He'd stay up with me at night, comforting me when another poor devil passed. We were never blessed with a daughter. Who will help them when I'm no longer here?' Huge tears rolled down her parchment-like cheeks, sliding into the crevices of her wrinkles.

'What happened to Giovanni?' Sara asked.

'His heart gave out.' Anna-Maria wiped the back of her hand across her face. 'One moment he was hammering a horseshoe on his anvil, the next he was flat on his back. They ran for me, but it was too late. He was stone-cold dead by the time I arrived. Even his soul was gone. I didn't get the chance to say goodbye. He was a good 'un, his soul went directly to a better place. No floating around in the ether weeping in despair for him, thank goodness.'

Sara didn't know what to say. All this talk of souls worried her. Perhaps Anna-Maria had caught a chill; it wouldn't surprise her. The cottage was cold and damp without the fire going, and if she hadn't gone to bed, it was no wonder the old woman was so confused.

The sound of water bubbling in the pot roused Sara from her thoughts. 'I'll make the tea now, you sit here and rest.'

She rummaged about in the cupboards until she found everything she needed, then took a tray with the tea and some stale biscuits over to Anna-Maria.

'Pop it on there,' the old woman said, pointing at a low table by the side of her armchair.

Sara put down the tray, then handed her the cup, and placed a biscuit on the saucer. 'They're a bit hard, but if you dip them in your tea they should be edible.'

'Thank you. Would you be so kind as to get that blanket and wrap it around me? My bones are aching today.'

Sara placed the blanket over Anna-Maria's legs, tucking it under her body to keep in the heat, then she got the fire going. Once it took hold, the room grew warmer.

The old woman leaned back and sighed. 'Ah, that feels better. It's been a long night.'

'I can imagine. Why on earth didn't you go back to bed?'

'The souls, they needed me.' Her voice trailed off and her eyelids drooped.

'Do you want me to go, so you can rest?'

'But you've only just got here, Ginevra. Why do you want to leave?' Anna-Maria suddenly sat up straight, frowning.

'No, I'm Sara, not Ginevra.'

A confused expression came over the old woman's face. 'Come now, Ginevra. I know we've had our differences, but that's all in the past. Stop being silly,' she said, a nervous tone creeping into her voice. Her hands shook, spilling some tea into the saucer.

Realisation dawned as Sara remembered Anna-Maria talking about having bad days. She lowered her voice. 'Come, drink your tea and eat some biscuits, then you can have a lie-down.'

'So then you can tell everyone I'm a crazy, foolish woman who speaks to ghosts?' Anna-Maria shouted, her eyes flashing with sudden anger. 'All because you're scared I'll let out your secret. Pah! As if I would. We're friends, remember? I've been by your side through everything and never said a word. I'm not about to start tattling now.' The cup dropped to the floor and cracked into several pieces, liquid spilling over the flagstones. Sara ignored it and took the old woman's hand, making shushing sounds to calm her down.

Anna-Maria gripped Sara's hand tightly in her own. 'You get out, Ginevra,' she hissed.

'I'm not Gi–' Sara said, but Anna-Maria was off in her own world and paid no attention.

'How long have we been friends? And as soon as you're with child, you spread rumours about me, telling everyone I'm crazy, because I know about you and the stable boy. You come across all high and mighty, the great healer, Ginevra Innocenti, from the villa up in the mountains, but you're not so grand now, are you? Not when the stable boy has planted his seed in your belly, and you have to pretend it's your husband's.'

Sara stepped back, her hand over her mouth. 'B-Bernardo?' she whispered.

'How many other stable boys do you have sniffing around you?' Anna-Maria's mouth curled into a sneer. 'Thanks to you spreading rumours, the only person in the village who'll speak to me is Giovanni. But at least my husband can be sure any *bambino* I carry is his.'

'No, it's not true,' Sara whimpered.

'You could have got rid of it, given the conte his own child.

We found the recipe, it would have been easy. But you refused, said you loved Bernardo and you could never kill his child, remember? And now it's too late, everyone knows there will be a new Innocenti in a few months.' She stopped, her chest heaving with emotion. 'I loved you, Ginevra, I would have done anything for you. I've worked by your side for years, brewing your potions. You helped me when I became the soul catcher, otherwise I would truly have gone crazy. Why? Why did you betray me like this?'

Sara stood, open-mouthed, her head spinning. Her grandmother had been pregnant with Bernardo's child! What had happened to it? Did her mother have a half-brother or sister somewhere? Maybe someone in the village had taken it, been paid to keep the secret and pretend the child was theirs. She had to find out, and only one person knew the truth.

'Wh-where is the child, Anna-Maria?'

'Eh?' The old woman peered up at her, and her body slumped back in the armchair as her anger dissipated.

'Ginevra's child. What happened to it?'

'What are you asking me for? You know what happened to her, Ginevra. She's up at the villa. Your husband's precious princess, the daughter of a stable boy. If only he knew. Hah.'

Sara somehow mumbled her goodbyes, promising to return the following morning, then fled from the cottage, sobbing wildly. She ran through the woods, avoiding the village and anyone she might bump into, her head pounding with all that she'd learned.

Mamma is Bernardo's daughter! The thought tormented her, filling her with horror. *She's not an Innocenti... and neither am I!* She stopped by a fallen tree and sat down, gasping for breath. *I'm not an Innocenti! I'm not a healer.* She put her head in her hands and wept, thinking about the last fight she'd had with her mother. *Does Mamma know? Is that why she didn't want me to come to the cottage? Because she knew I could never become a healer?*

Then another thought occurred to her. *Bernardo lied. He and my grandmother were lovers before my mother was born, not after!*

13

Sara flung the cottage door open and stormed inside, not caring about the muddy trail she left behind on the tiled floor.

'My mother knew, didn't she?' she yelled. She threw herself at Bernardo, her fists thumping on his chest, arms, shoulders, anywhere she could land a punch. He didn't defend himself at first, but as her efforts became stronger, he gripped her arms and pushed her away. Sara fell backwards, staggering as if she were drunk. She managed to regain her balance, her body trembling as anger surged through her.

'You lied to me!' she shouted, breathing heavily. 'You said it was that one time, after my grandfather beat her, but it wasn't, was it? You and Nonna were lovers long before that!' Bernardo held out his hands towards her in supplication, but she slapped them away. 'Why? Why didn't you tell me the truth?'

'I didn't want to upset you,' Bernardo said hesitantly. 'I, we... yes, we were lovers, but then she married your grandfather, she had to, she was with child and couldn't marry me. Your mother found out by accident.' He hung his head, unable to look her in the eye.

'That's why Mamma hates me, isn't it?' Spit flew from her mouth as she spoke, but she was beyond caring. 'She knows, and every time she looks at me, she's reminded of her peasant origins!'

'She doesn't hate you,' he said, his voice weak from emotion. 'She hates the healers, and the curse on the family, but she cares for you.'

'That's why she sent me away from the villa,' Sara said bitterly. 'Because she cares for me.'

'How did you find out? Did Anna-Maria tell you? I know she was upset with Ginevra after they fell out, but this is a spiteful thing to do, even for her.'

'She was having a bad day and thought I was my grandmother; she merely told me a few home truths. Ginevra hurt her back then. She told everyone Anna-Maria was crazy, so they wouldn't believe her if she happened to mention who my mother's father really was. It would seem my grandmother wasn't the lovely person you said she was. I'm ashamed to be related to her, her behaviour was worse than any peasant's. And you condoned it.' A sneer crept into her voice.

Bernardo stood as still as a statue, a hurt expression on his face. When he spoke, his voice was quiet. 'Your grandmother was a good woman, I'm sorry you think this way about her. And I may be a mere peasant, Sara, but you and your mother are descendants of a long line of healers, a lineage more noble than that of any king or queen. Your grandfather may have been a conte, but your true birthright comes from your grandmother. The name Innocenti has been passed from mother to daughter since the first healer wrote her name in the book. Since then no healer has taken her husband's name – once an Innocenti, always an Innocenti, that's what your grandmother used to say. I'm sorry you feel that your lineage has been contaminated by my peasant blood, but at least I can hold my head up high and say I loved your grandmother with all my heart and would never have laid a finger on her.'

Sara hardly heard his words, her anger suppressing any rational thought. 'I hate you,' she hissed. 'You've ruined everything. You let me believe I could do this, live here and become a healer, and instead it was all lies.' She turned and ran out of the cottage, ignoring his shouts behind her.

She fled across the clearing and into the woods, not caring where she was going; she wanted to get as far away as possible. Branches and brambles tore at her arms and legs, leaving stinging scratches. She ran through a clump of nettles before she realised they were there, but barely felt the burning welts on her skin. She came to a halt, panting heavily, and leaned against a tree. As her breathing subsided, she could hear the soft murmuring of a nearby river and birds singing in the trees.

Hardly aware of what she was doing, she walked towards the water. She'd never gone so far into the woods before and didn't recognise her surroundings. She found herself standing on the banks of a fast-flowing river, its waters crystal clear. Dragonflies, butterflies, bees and a myriad of insects filled the air, zooming low over the water or flitting through the undergrowth. She watched, spellbound, as they went about their business without a care in the world.

A sudden noise startled her, and she spun around to see the tail of a fox disappear into some bushes. Intrigued, she pushed her way through the undergrowth – the welts on her legs stung, and she was relieved to see there weren't any nettles there – and burst into a tiny glade where the trees created a canopy with their branches overhead. She stopped in front of a grave, her hand over her mouth in shock, and took a tentative step forward. The inscription on the headstone was covered in moss and partially eroded by the weather, but she could make out the year. 1349. She rubbed at the marble, clearing away the moss, and peered closely at the inscription. *Bob. Faithful friend, in life and death.*

She felt a quiet calm come over her there in the glade, the sun's rays penetrating the branches of the trees to create a green-tinged gloom. A dragonfly was sitting on the headstone – *her* dragonfly, a small voice whispered in her head – its wings twitching against its body as if it were impatient to be off. She reached over and touched the old marble, its cool freshness soothing against her skin. A wonderful, calm feeling washed over her and the anger left her body as quickly as it had arrived. She sank down onto the ground, soft grass cushioning her knees, and leaned her forehead against the headstone. A quiet voice began speaking inside her head, and she listened carefully.

It spoke of its past, of a terrible sickness that had devastated the continent, of a journey across a vast sea to this place, of evil and murder, and of love and healing. It told her of the Innocenti, how generation after generation had worked their healing magic for people near and far, of tragic events and persecution, of finding the strength and courage to continue their work, despite their tribulations. She listened as it listed the healers, one by one, telling her about the adversities they'd had to face while the curse placed on the land became stronger and spread its evil. The curse the voice had died for, during its creation.

Tears poured down her cheeks as she heard its words and understood what her grandmother had been through; what all the healers had been through. Her family's history was tragic and often violent, interspersed with briefly happy moments in time, and she understood that her grandmother had been the last in a long line of courageous women battling against the harshest odds.

Why shouldn't Ginevra have taken the chance for some happiness when the occasion presented itself? the voice asked her. *Perhaps Bernardo was meant to carry on the Innocenti lineage and father the next healer. Your grandmother never had any other children after your mother. She paid for that happiness every day of her life, and died not knowing if there would ever be another healer. Bernardo gave you life, yes, but your grandmother gave you knowledge. Use it well.*

Sara opened her eyes, surprised to find the afternoon light had given way to dusk. Creatures scuttled through the undergrowth, hurrying home before night fell. How long had she been there? She got up, her legs stiff from kneeling for so long, and brushed the dirt from her knees. The dragonfly flitted over, hovering before her face for a moment, its dark bulbous eyes gleaming as it regarded her.

'I know,' Sara said. 'I have to go back and say I'm sorry, right?'

'Talking to yourself, Sara?' Bernardo said from behind her.

Sara whirled round, the dragonfly forgotten. 'Wh-where did you come from?'

'I got worried when you didn't come back and followed your tracks through the forest. It wasn't difficult, there were bits of material stuck on brambles and the grass was all trampled.' Sara glanced down at her dress, noticing the small rips for the first time. 'I thought I'd see you before I go.' He shifted the bag slung over his shoulder.

'Go?'

'You're right. I've ruined your life, and your mother's. I should have told you so you could make your decision knowing all the facts. Instead, I put those ideas of becoming a healer into your head and ruined your future. I'll ask Rosa to put in a good word for you with the contessa, maybe she'll take you back.'

'No.' Sara surprised herself with the determination in her voice. 'I'm the one who should be apologising to you. I was angry and said things I should never have said. Will you forgive me?'

'I should be the one asking for forgiveness.' Bernardo

lowered his bag to the ground and stepped towards her. 'We have a lot to talk about.'

'Yes, we do.' Sara flung her arms around him, her tears soaking his shirt. 'Nonno,' she mumbled.

He snorted. 'Nonno. That's going to take some getting used to. I thought not calling you Lady Sara was hard enough.'

'You'd better get used to it, Nonno,' Sara said, half laughing and half crying. She wiped her tears with the back of her hand. 'Shall we go home?'

'Maybe we'll avoid the nettles this time,' he said, pointing at the red marks on her legs.

She rubbed them, wincing at the pain. 'I'm sure we've got a remedy for that, haven't we?'

'If we haven't, we'll make one. In the meantime, you can use some of these.' Bernardo gathered some dock leaves and gave them to her.

Sara rubbed them on the welts, giving a small sigh of relief as the stinging subsided.

Bernardo smiled at her and held out his hand. 'Come, granddaughter. Let's go home.'

As they left the glade, Sara turned to look at the grave a last time. 'Do you know who's buried here?'

Bernardo shrugged. 'No idea. Your grandmother never mentioned there was a grave in the woods, maybe she didn't know. Why?'

'No reason. He just seems someone with a sensible head on his shoulders.'

Bernardo glanced questioningly at her but said nothing. She took hold of his hand again and followed him back through the woods to the cottage.

14

The fire crackled in the hearth, the flames casting a cosy glow into the room. Bernardo picked up his drink, the glass glinting in the half light, and gently swirled the amber liquid.

'Bit o' luck, finding that bottle of brandy.' He took a long, appreciative sniff. 'Thank you, Ginevra, my love.'

Sara sipped her drink, blinking as the brandy hit the back of her throat and travelled down to her stomach. A warm feeling settled over her and she relaxed, the tension from the day's events dissipating.

'Will you tell me more about her?' she asked, making herself comfortable in the armchair.

'Your grandmother?'

Sara nodded. 'In the woods, the voice said—' She stopped, afraid she was starting to sound as crazy as Anna-Maria.

'The voice said what?' Bernardo smiled at her.

She took courage from his kind expression. 'The voice said that Nonna deserved a chance at happiness. Was her life really so miserable?'

'When I first arrived at the villa, your grandmother was like a ray of sunshine. She was so full of energy, she rose early in the morning and didn't stop until she went to bed at night. Her mother despaired of her ever finding a husband; Ginevra lived and breathed horses, all day and every day. She was always down at the stables, and rode most days.'

Sara half closed her eyes, trying to imagine her grandmother as a young, headstrong woman.

'You remind me of her a lot.' Bernardo took another mouthful of brandy. 'Ginevra was admired by every man in the neighbourhood, and some from further beyond. Many asked for her hand in marriage, but she turned down every one. I thought she was being fickle, until the day I found out the reason why.'

Sara glanced at him. 'You?'

He frowned, his bushy grey eyebrows almost meeting in the middle. The wrinkles on his leathery face appeared deeper in the firelight, grief ingrained in each crevice. 'It was a few months after I started accompanying her on rides. She'd challenged me to a race, as usual, and set off at a mad gallop. That black devil of a stallion was the fastest horse in the stables, there was no chance my mare would keep up with it. When I caught up with her, she looked so beautiful sat atop that black devil pawing at the ground that all I could do was gawp at her. Her cheeks were flushed red, her hair all tangled and wild, and those green eyes sparkled with mirth. She had no idea how beautiful she was.'

'You really loved her,' Sara whispered, tears welling up in her eyes.

'And I thought I was doomed to love her from afar.' He shook his head. 'As I drew near, I thought she would laugh at how slow I was, like she usually did. But she remained silent, her face serious, and beckoned me to pull up alongside her. I can still remember the scent of sweat coming off the horses, mixed with the sweet perfume she always wore and the fragrance of her freshly washed hair; all so familiar, yet at the same time it was as if a stranger stood before me.'

Sara watched her grandfather as he reminisced, the brandy forgotten on the table beside her. She wished she could have known him back then, before old age had wreaked its effects on him.

'She leaned over and kissed me, full on the lips.' Bernardo chuckled. 'You could say I was shocked! But she tasted so sweet, and it seemed so right.' His voice faded. 'We were young, and when she said she loved me, well, it felt like I'd died and gone to heaven.' He smiled sadly at Sara. 'Sometimes I think it would have been better if I had. We spent every spare moment together, every chance we got to be alone. It was inevitable, really.'

'What was?' Sara could hardly breathe.

'A couple of months later she told me she was with child. My child.'

'Oh.'

'Oh, indeed. We were so young, so sure that our love would overcome every obstacle, even the fact that I was a stable boy. But we were wrong. Before she even had a chance to speak to her parents, they told her they'd found a husband and she was to be married in a few weeks. She was distraught, she threatened to kill herself if they forced her to marry against her will, but they wouldn't be moved.' He sighed. 'I think they suspected something was going on between us, and had decided to put a stop to it before it was too late.'

'But it was already too late.'

'Yes. She wanted us to run away together, get married and live our lives away from the villa, the cottage, everything she'd ever known. I got carried away with her eagerness and we almost did it, but in the end I couldn't let her ruin her future like that.'

'But she would have been happy.' Tears rolled down Sara's cheeks at the thought of her grandparents' love being destroyed.

'Would she?' Bernardo finished his brandy and put the glass on the floor. 'Never to tend the Grove again, never to be a healer anymore – would that have made her happy? Or would she have grown to hate me for taking her away from her destiny? The hardest thing I've ever done was telling Ginevra to marry your grandfather, il Marchese di Lucca, before it became evident she was with child. She vowed never to have anything more to do with me. It broke my heart.'

'You didn't see her after that?'

'She couldn't keep away from the stables, but she avoided me as much as possible for many months. I accepted her punishment, it was nothing less than I deserved. Her wedding day was the grandest event we'd seen in many years, all pomp and splendour. But she changed afterwards. She appeared subdued, her feistiness and spirit faded until they were barely visible. Beaten out of her, as I discovered afterwards. Ludovico was a violent man, a bully. He knew that the child wasn't his, but she wouldn't tell him whose it was, and he made her suffer for it for the rest of her life.

'She eventually forgave me, although our friendship was never the same after. She sought refuge here at the cottage, and would pass her days preparing her remedies for the villagers. I would catch a glimpse of her every now and then, when she came to the stables, and I saw the bruises on her arms that she tried to hide. I wanted to take her away from that brute, but where would we have gone? And once your mother was born, it was impossible. I had to hold my tongue and watch, impotent, as he tried to bend her to his will. And every bruise she got for disobeying him was like a stab to my heart.' Bernardo took a deep, shuddering breath. 'She never gave in to him, not completely. Even after he forbade her to come to the cottage, she found a way to defy him. She refused to stop being a healer.'

'And my mother saw him beat her?'

'I think so, yes. He was a loud, arrogant man who shouted at the servants for the slightest thing, and the atmosphere at the villa was always tense, I was told.'

Sara remained silent for a while. 'I suppose I can understand why my mother turned her back on becoming a healer,' she said eventually. 'But how did she become so cold-hearted and bitter towards everyone? Even me.'

'Fear is a powerful weapon, Sara. It can beat down the strongest person. Ludovico ruled with a rod of iron, no one dared stand in his way. Not even Ginevra. Lucrezia didn't have your grandmother's strength.'

Sara tried to feel compassion for her mother, but found she couldn't. 'I can never forgive her,' she said bitterly. 'What she witnessed that day was terrible, yes, but Grandfa– Ludovico has been dead for many years now. Even if she didn't want to take over from Nonna, she could have let me do it. Why is she so against me becoming a healer?'

'Perhaps she fears for your safety. Ludovico's threats were very real in those times, and still stand today.'

'The villagers speak about my grandmother with fondness, they remember how kind she was and how she helped them. Surely that is better than the unrest there is now, and the bitterness the villagers have towards my family?'

'Sometimes I find it hard to believe Lucrezia is my daughter,' Bernardo said sadly. 'Unfortunately, she has taken much from Ludovico and little from me. But now, we have a new healer, if you would like to take the position.'

'There's no reason for me not to, is there?' Sara said, her heart beating faster at the thought.

'On the contrary, I think it could help settle the troubles

down in the village,' he replied gravely. 'The locals are angry with your parents, and this could be one way to placate them.'

'What's going on? No one will tell me.'

'It's nothing that can't be solved. It'll pass, as these things always do.'

Sara narrowed her eyes, but didn't press him further. 'Tomorrow morning I'll go back to Anna-Maria. If she's better, I'll ask her to start teaching me.'

'Are you sure?' Bernardo raised an eyebrow. 'Last time you went, you came back like a storm from hell!'

Sara blushed. 'It was a shock, that's all. I wasn't upset.'

He burst out laughing. 'Thank goodness. I'd hate to see you when you're really angry!' He got up with a groan. 'I don't know about you, but I'm about ready for my bed.'

Sara gathered the glasses and took them over to the sink. 'Thank you, Nonno.'

'For what?' He stopped on the stairs, hand gripping the banister, and looked down at her.

'For everything,' she replied softly. 'Goodnight.'

''Night.'

She watched him make his way upstairs, glad he had gone to find her instead of leaving without saying a word. She couldn't imagine life without him.

15

Sara found Anna-Maria in her kitchen when she arrived the next morning.

'Come in, come in,' she called at Sara's timid knock. 'Oh, child, it's you. I wondered if you would come back. Come, have a seat.'

'How are you feeling today?' Sara asked as she sat down on one of the wooden chairs. She studied the old woman and was pleased to see a more lucid expression on her face.

Anna-Maria sat on the other chair and rested her hands on the table. 'I'm sorry for yesterday. It happens when I have to tend the souls. I can hardly remember who I am afterwards, let alone anyone who comes to visit me. I thought you were your grandmother.' She fell silent.

Sara took the old woman's gnarled hands in hers. 'It's all right. It was a shock, I have to admit, and I was upset, but I'm all right now. Bernardo and I have talked, I understand everything.'

'I get confused. The spirits told me many things that night. They spoke of a darkness that is coming to blight our land. I saw terrible things, created from hate and ignorance. I was sad and tired, and when I saw you, I thought Ginevra had come back.' Anna-Maria shook her head. 'The souls use up all my energy when I send them on, it leaves me drained. The look on your face when I told you about Ginevra carrying Bernardo's child. I'm so sorry.'

'I was angry at first. I shouted at Bernardo, and told him to leave, then ran into the forest to get away from him.'

'But you said everything is all right.' Anna-Maria pulled her hands away, a bewildered look on her face.

'I was so angry, I didn't know what to do. Then I came across a glade I'd never seen before, with a grave in it.'

'Go on.' The old woman leaned forward, staring at her intently.

'I felt such serenity there, as if I'd found a haven where I could leave all my troubles behind me. There was a voice, and it told me so many things, about the healers and the Innocenti, and a curse here on the land.'

'Bob.' Anna-Maria gazed off into the distance, and Sara thought for a moment she'd lost her again. 'The grave has been there for countless centuries, and Bob has helped many healers who lost their way. Your grandmother took me there once to see if I could save his soul, but his is not a soul that needs saving. He will stay there for eternity, giving advice when sought, his words a comfort when everything seems dark and desperate. Heed his words, Sara.'

'Who is he?' Sara whispered.

'No one knows. His name isn't mentioned in the book, but from the date on the grave, Ginevra thought that he must have come here with Agnes.'

'Agnes?'

'The first healer. Her name is written in Ginevra's book, you must have seen it.'

Sara shook her head. 'Mamma has the book, she won't give it

to me. That's why I need you to teach me the remedies, remember?'

'Ah, yes, you did say. You should ask her to give it to you, it's your heritage and your right.' Anna-Maria tutted, and stood up. 'Come. We must pick fresh herbs if I'm to teach you anything today. Get that basket and come with me to the garden.'

It was a glorious day. White clouds scudded across the clear blue sky, the flowers, trees, and grass sparkled in the sun's rays, and the wildlife took advantage of the warm weather. A gentle breeze kept them cool as they worked, and soon the wicker basket was filled with aromatic cuttings.

Back inside Anna-Maria's cottage, they cut and prepared the herbs, soaking some in warm water, boiling others, then straining off the concoction and pouring it into glass bottles. By midday they had a row of bottles filled with a pleasant-smelling brew.

Sara sniffed. 'It smells wonderful, much better than mine and Bernardo's attempts so far. What is it for?'

'This helps women's monthly problems, takes away the cramps and lessens the bleeding.'

'Ah. And the willow bark helps with pain and headaches?'

'Good. Now, using this and adding some beeswax, olive oil and almond oil, we're going to make an unguent that will help muscle pains.'

'Bernardo could use that,' Sara said, smiling. 'He keeps complaining about his back.'

'Then you can give it to him and see what he thinks.' Anna-Maria stretched, and grimaced with pain. 'Aching joints is a part of old age, I'm afraid. I'm glad you came to me, you have given me purpose again and made me see there's more to life than that old tree and passing souls. Thank you.'

Sara hesitated. 'Will you tell me about my grandmother? From when you were friends, I mean. I know so little about her, only what Bernardo has told me, really. If you feel like it,' she added, not wanting to upset the old woman.

Anna-Maria chuckled. 'Of course. Where to start? She was so mischievous when she was little, always getting into trouble. The first time I saw her was in the village square. She was only five years old, and was stuck up a tree she'd climbed for a dare. They had the devil of a time getting her back down, goodness knows how she got up there. My mamma looked after her until some servants arrived from the villa to take her back, and I sat with her. I was a couple of years older, but I was tongue-tied in front of someone from the "big house", as we called it. It was like sitting in the presence of royalty!'

The old woman's eyes sparkled as she told Sara tale after tale about her grandmother, talking all the time they worked.

The days passed and Sara learned everything she could from Anna-Maria. After a while, she could go out into the garden and pick any herb the old woman told her to collect, without any uncertainty. She made sure she said her prayer of thanks while taking what she needed from each plant, and the cuttings were treated with care. She learned the different methods of preparing the concoctions, and which herbs would treat which malady. She was a gifted student, seemingly drawing on knowledge she'd carried inside her until this moment.

Bernardo tried the unguent they'd made, and was delighted with the results. 'I haven't felt this good in years!' He flexed his back and making a few tentative jumps. 'Feels like it did twenty years ago.' He winced, and grabbed his side. 'Well, maybe five.'

Every morning, Anna-Maria taught her a new recipe and every afternoon Sara returned to the cottage and prepared her own remedies, using everything she'd learned. She picked the ingredients she needed in the Grove, and soon the sweet aroma of boiling herbs wafted throughout the cottage from morning to night. She loved to visit the pantry and see its shelves loaded with glass bottles and pots.

Now that they knew the remedies would work, they decided to let the villagers know that a healer was once more in residence at the cottage. A few people trickled in at first, only one or two a day, then more, curious to see the new healer for themselves. They brought bread, chickens, vegetables from their own gardens, or household items they'd made themselves, in exchange for the remedies for their various ailments. They'd chat about anything and everything as they sipped tea and ate the biscuits Sara had made, reminiscing about the old days before everything had gone bad.

'The villagers don't seem very happy,' Sara remarked one evening to Bernardo. It had been a long day, and they had both been glad when the last person left and they could finally sit down and rest.

He took a long puff of his pipe, leaning back as he blew the smoke towards the ceiling. 'There is a lot of bad feeling at the moment,' he said carefully.

'Bad feeling? About?'

'It's just that your parents...' He glanced at her, and hesitated.

Sara shifted uncomfortably in her armchair. 'Carry on. My parents, what?'

'Your parents aren't hiring as many people as before. They've gone in for these new-fangled farming methods, machines powered by steam and the like, and hiring cheaper labour from the coast, so the villagers here are without work. They're even getting rid of the horses, and only keeping those they need for pulling the machines.'

'But the Innocenti are famous for their stables! What on earth are they thinking of?' Sara was dismayed at this latest news. She could only imagine how Bernardo felt, those horses had been his life.

'You know them better than I do. All I know is that people aren't happy. Which is why it's a good thing you've decided to become a healer. Right now, you're all those people have got. Otherwise they'd be dying of the simplest ailments, all because they haven't got money to pay the doctor.'

Sara glanced over at the kitchen, the cupboards groaning under the weight of the foodstuffs the locals had brought them in exchange for their cures. She made up her mind in an instant. 'Right. From now on, we no longer accept payment.'

Bernardo raised an eyebrow. 'And what are we supposed to live on. Thin air?'

'Let me finish. You know the villagers, you know which ones are suffering the most. Those people mustn't pay a thing, not even a loaf of bread. Understood? It's more important their children eat than us. We have our vegetables and chickens here, we'll get by. We'll only accept gifts from those who can afford it, and only when we need something.' She clenched her fists, her chest heaving with emotion.

Bernardo removed the pipe from his mouth. 'Your grandmother would be so proud of you,' he said, visibly moved. Sara was sure she could see tears glistening in his eyes. '*I'm* proud of you.'

'It's the least I can do, to rectify my parents' actions,' she replied, her heart breaking at the thought of the villagers without work. She had no idea why her parents were doing this, but she would do her best to help the people of Gallicano.

16

JULY 1884

S ara sat on the edge of the marble fountain in the Grove, a cup of steaming tea in her hand, and breathed in the aromatic scents of the plants around her. There was a fresh breeze at that time of the morning, the sun peeking over the tops of the mountains, not yet at full strength, and she often sat there alone. It was her time to put her thoughts in order, and prepare herself for the day ahead. She took a sip of tea and waited for the dragonfly to arrive, as it inevitably did.

So much had changed since she'd decided to become a healer four years earlier. Bernardo had restored the cottage as much as he was able; the roof no longer leaked whenever it rained, and smoke no longer filled the living room whenever they lit the chimney. His vegetable patch was thriving, they had enough food to last all through the long winters, and the animals kept them supplied with everything else they needed. Times were getting harder for the people in the mountains; more and more of the illnesses she was treating were caused by malnutrition and depression, and she often cursed her parents for their callousness towards the locals.

She remembered those first months, when she had little

confidence in her skills and had to learn everything from Anna-Maria. Sara's abilities had slowly taken over, until she instinctively knew which plants were the best remedy for most illnesses. Nowadays she rarely had to call on Anna-Maria's help, although the old woman insisted on being her assistant, as she had been for Ginevra many years before. Sara had passed many pleasant evenings at the cottage with Anna-Maria and Bernardo, listening to their tales of times gone by.

'Do you remember when Ginevra...?' Anna-Maria would start, and Bernardo would join in enthusiastically, the three of them laughing at some of her grandmother's more outrageous behaviour.

'Lucrezia used to love jumping in puddles,' Anna-Maria said one day.

Sara giggled. 'Really?'

'Yes. The deeper and muddier, the better. This was when she was just a little girl, of course.'

'Of course.' Sara found it hard to imagine her mother as a young child, laughing and carefree as she stomped her way through dirty puddles. She tried to compare the image with the rigid, stern-faced woman she'd always known, and shook her head. Anna-Maria had many more stories about Lucrezia, and Sara noticed Bernardo listening, fascinated. He had missed much of her childhood, working in the stables and rarely going up to the villa. His daughter had never shown much interest in horses, preferring to stay indoors and preserve her pale complexion. Sara felt saddened at how much he had lost over the years.

She finished her tea, stood, and smoothed down her apron. The dragonfly hovered before her; she stretched out her hand towards it, then sighed as a bell rang from the cottage, their signal that a customer had arrived.

'Another morning, perhaps,' she said to the dragonfly, and

watched as it flitted away. Gathering her skirts, she straightened her shoulders and went back to the cottage.

'Signora Bonomi, good morning! What can I do for you today?'

'As I've told you before, call me Loretta,' she replied. 'Signora Bonomi makes me feel old! I'm sorry I came so early, you must still be having breakfast.'

'Not at all. I'm an early riser, always up with the larks, me.' Sara smiled and helped the limping woman to a chair, where she sat down gingerly. She took in the woman's pallid face, the dark shadows under her eyes, and her skinny frame, and wondered what hardships she was going through. She was barely twenty-five, only five years older than Sara herself, but with four children and a husband out of work, life couldn't be easy for her.

'Here, drink this.' Sara handed Loretta a steaming mug of her special herbal tea, with two spoonfuls of honey added. There was always a pot of boiling water on the stove, ready for her patients, and a tea for every need.

'Hmm, that's so good.' Loretta took a sip, wrapping her hands around the cup to warm them. Sara was worried; it was the height of summer and even though the cottage was cool, it wasn't cold by any means.

'You get that down you, then we can talk,' she said brightly. She busied herself putting away some bottles she had washed earlier, while Loretta drank her tea.

'Here, thank you,' she said gratefully, passing the cup to Sara. She leaned back, wincing in pain.

Sara got a stool and sat down in front of her. 'Now, tell me what's wrong.'

Loretta's eyes filled with tears. 'He didn't mean to do it,' she sobbed, rubbing her back. 'He found out about the baby.'

Sara handed her a clean handkerchief. 'Tell me from the beginning.'

The woman took a couple of deep, shuddering breaths, and dabbed at her eyes. 'I-I hadn't had me monthlies for a while, so I knew I was with child – again. We've already got the four of them, and can't cope as it is. But I had to tell him. So yesterday, while they were all at their grandmother's, I spoke to him.'

'He didn't take it too well,' Sara said.

'No. He shouted at me, asking how we're going to feed them all, saying we can't afford another one. I told him we'd manage somehow, we always do. He said I was stupid, there's no work to be had anywhere, and without work there's no food. I started crying, and he hit me to shut me up. It was me own fault.' Her voice trailed off.

'Where did he hit you?'

'Me back, stomach, legs, everywhere,' Loretta whispered. 'I bled overnight, although it's stopped now.' She put her hand over her stomach. 'Have I lost it?'

'Come.' Sara helped her stand up. 'Let's go up to my room where it's more private and we'll see what's happening.'

Loretta lay on her side on Sara's bed and lifted her smock. Sara sucked in a breath when she saw the mottled bruises over her back and legs. She gently turned her over and grimaced when she saw two round bruises on her stomach.

'Babies are tough little things, they can withstand a bump or two,' she said, trying to reassure the woman.

'But what if he's damaged it?' Loretta asked anxiously. 'Me sister, she fell down some stairs in the early days. She didn't lose the baby, but when it was born its head was all misshapen and its eyes went in different directions. It lived for a few years, but it didn't have much of a life. I couldn't bear it if this one–' She burst into tears.

Sara didn't know what to do. She had helped women give birth over the last few years and given them concoctions during their confinement to help with various complaints, but she didn't consider herself an expert yet. She knew that Anna-Maria had helped her grandmother on many occasions; she would have to ask her.

'Will you wait here while I go to speak to a friend?' she said to Loretta.

'Who? How long? I left the children with me mother.' She struggled to sit up, then collapsed, panting.

'Please, stay calm. Lie here and rest, I'll be as quick as I can. I need to get some advice.'

Sara hurried out of the room and down the stairs. Bernardo was outside, chopping logs for firewood.

'Nonno, I need to go to the village and ask Anna-Maria something. I've left Signora Bonomi in my room, she needs to remain lying down and rest. Don't let her go home.'

'Something wrong, Sara?'

'I hope not, but I don't know enough about these things. If anyone else turns up, ask them to come back tomorrow.'

'Don't worry, I'll keep an eye on things here.'

Sara hurried across the clearing, fearful she wouldn't get back in time to save the baby.

17

Anna-Maria insisted on going to the cottage with Sara. 'I need to see her before I can say either way,' she said, gathering some things and putting them in her basket. She handed it to Sara to carry.

She blanched when she saw which herbs the old woman had collected. 'Aren't they for aborting?'

'Yes. Like I said, we don't know what we'll need,' Anna-Maria said sharply. 'If there's any risk either to the mother or the child, this may be for the best.'

They walked back to the cottage in silence, both lost in their thoughts. Bernardo greeted them as they went indoors.

'She was sleeping about ten minutes ago when I went to check on her,' he said. 'Here, give me that basket.' He took it from Sara and put it on the kitchen table.

'Right, let's go and see her,' Anna-Maria said.

Sara led the way upstairs, Anna-Maria huffing and puffing as she followed. Loretta was asleep on the bed; her eyes opened as they entered the room.

'Loretta, this is my friend, Anna-Maria. She's going to have a look at you.'

The woman drew back, her eyes wide in fear. 'The soul catcher?'

'That's right, but hopefully there'll be no souls to catch today,' Anna-Maria answered. 'Lift your dress so I can have a look.'

Sara nodded reassuringly, and Loretta pulled up her dress. She winced as the old woman prodded at her bruises, then yelped when she touched her stomach.

'I'm going to have to push a bit. It's going to hurt, but that can't be helped,' Anna-Maria said. 'How far along are you?'

Loretta thought for a moment. 'About five months, I reckon.'

Sara gasped. 'Five months? And you only told your husband yesterday?'

She shrugged. 'I was fearful of his reaction. And I thought I might lose it, happens all the time in the early months.'

'You hoped it'd go away by itself, isn't that so?' Anna-Maria said kindly.

Loretta sniffed, tears rolling down her cheeks. 'Just me luck it didn't,' she mumbled.

Anna-Maria rolled her hands expertly over Loretta's stomach, making her cry out in pain. Sara waited by her side, wishing she could do something to help the distressed woman.

'I can't feel anything,' Anna-Maria said eventually.

'That's good, right?' Loretta said eagerly.

The old woman shook her head. 'I mean, I can't feel *anything*. Not even its soul.'

'It's... dead?' Loretta whimpered, her eyes wide open.

Anna-Maria took hold of her hands and nodded. 'But it's still inside you, so we need to give you something to make it come out.' She turned to Sara and quietly explained what she needed.

Loretta started wailing, a terrible, keening noise that echoed throughout the house. Sara and Anna-Maria carried out their tasks in silence, bearing Loretta's pain as if it were their own, then held her until she finally fell asleep, exhausted.

❧

'You need to give her a tea made from these herbs, with lots of honey to give her strength,' Anna-Maria told Sara when they were back in the kitchen. 'Let her sleep, then accompany her home.'

'What do I tell her husband?'

'The truth. That she lost the baby, and she needs time to recover.' Anna-Maria thumped her fist on the table, her face twisted with grief. 'Maybe burying his dead child will make him think twice before raising his hands to a woman again.'

Sara shuddered at the thought of the little bundle they'd placed in a basket in the corner of her room. Perfect in every way, the baby boy was a little smaller than her hand. He hadn't had a chance of living, Anna-Maria had whispered to her, his soul had fled long before Loretta gave birth.

They'd let her hold him for a while, standing in silence as she'd poured her grief out over his tiny body.

'We must take him to the priest for burial.' Sara had reached to take the baby, but Loretta had refused to let him go.

'Please, let me take him home, back where he belongs. We'll put him in the garden, underneath the apple tree the kids love so much, and I can go and talk to him whenever I want.'

Sara had glanced at Anna-Maria, who gave her a slight nod. 'All right,' she'd said, unable to deny Loretta something that would give her solace in the years to come. Her heart broke at the thought of the poor woman upstairs, asleep in her bed.

Bernardo passed a bowl of broth and some bread to Anna-Maria. 'Here, eat this before you leave. We don't want you taking ill as well.' He sat down at the table with them. 'Things are getting worse in the village. With no work, people are suffering. The men are angry, and that makes them hit out.'

'That's no excuse,' Anna-Maria snapped, chewing on a piece of bread.

'No, there's never any excuse for beating your wife,' Bernardo replied. 'But you're seeing more of this sort of thing lately and it's going to get worse, I reckon, if things don't get better around here.'

'Maybe I should talk to my parents,' Sara suggested. 'Tell them how the villagers are suffering, beg my father to give them work so at least the children won't starve.'

Anna-Maria snorted. 'You haven't seen them for years. Do you really think they're going to welcome you back and listen to you preaching to them how to run their estate? You're more naïve than I thought.'

'I have to try,' Sara said, although she knew in her heart Anna-Maria was right.

18

Sara watched the woman scurry across the square to the bakery. She left the shade of the cherry tree and slowly followed, giving her time to make her purchases. As she reached the shop, the woman came out.

'Good morning, Rosa,' Sara said.

'Lady Sara, you gave me a fright,' Rosa replied, flustered. She glanced around, then grabbed Sara's hand. 'You must be careful, others from the villa may see us talking.'

'I need to speak with you,' Sara said, matching Rosa's tones.

'Not here.' Rosa fiddled with her basket, tucking the cloth over the bread she'd bought.

'Come to the cottage,' Sara pleaded.

'You know I can't.' Rosa thought for a moment. 'The cemetery of St. Jacopo's, hardly anyone goes there at this time of day. It should be safe. I'll go first, you follow in a few minutes.'

Sara nodded, and Rosa scuttled away. She waited a while, then strolled through the streets, slowly making her way up the steep incline to the church overlooking the village. She stopped and talked with some of the villagers, listening carefully as they described their latest ailments to her, to which she suggested treatments, telling them to visit the cottage when they could.

At long last she reached the cemetery and stepped through the gate, closing it behind her. She could see Rosa over in the far corner, sat on a bench under some cypress trees.

'I can't stay long,' Rosa told her as Sara approached. 'I'm expected back soon.'

'I appreciate you waiting for me. I wanted to ask what's going on up at the villa. The situation in the village is getting worse, people are starting to starve down here. Why have my parents done this?'

'They've changed.' Rosa's face was grave. 'Ever since you left, they've become completely different people. Your father no longer travels, but has taken over the running of the estate. He sent away the steward, Giuseppe, saying he could run things more efficiently, but the truth is, the estate has been going downhill ever since. He won't hire men from the village anymore, as he claims they steal from him. Instead, he has brought in workers from the coast, who know how to use those steam-powered machines he's bought. But the machines don't work properly on our steep slopes, and any fool can see his crops have suffered; these new men have no idea how to farm up here in the mountains.'

Sara was shocked. 'And my mother? Doesn't she try to change his mind?'

'Hah!' Rosa folded her arms and leaned back against the tree trunk. 'It was your mother's idea to close the stables. All those beautiful horses, gone. It would break Bernardo's heart. And obviously, all the stable boys, grooms, coachmen, they're gone too. She's kept one pair of carriage horses and one coachman for when she goes visiting, and a couple of draft horses, that's all. Everyone cried when they came to take the animals away, it was heartbreaking.'

'But why would they do this? It doesn't make sense.'

'To punish the villagers,' Rosa replied, gazing at a spot on the ground.

'Punish them for what?' Sara asked, but she was beginning to understand.

'When they sent you away, they thought you'd be back within a few weeks, a month at most, begging for their forgiveness. When you didn't, they sent servants to find out why. And they discovered you were not only a healer, but already popular with the locals, who swore by your cures.'

'Why are they so cruel?' Sara's eyes filled with tears.

'Your mother hates the healers. She saw her own mother threatened by the other landowners, who claimed she was a witch and wanted to lock her away in an asylum. Your great-grandmother told her stories of past healers who had been burned at the stake, or stoned to death, or ostracised from society, all because they wanted to help make people better. She was terrified that the same thing could happen to her, so refused to even consider becoming a healer. Deep down, she was scared for you too, but then she saw you doing well, becoming a favourite with the villagers, and this has stirred up all the hate and bitterness she has inside. She doesn't want you to succeed, as this will prove she was wrong and her mother was right, so she has decided to punish the villagers instead.'

'By starving them?' Sara twisted her hands in anguish. 'I'm trying to help these poor people as much as I can, but we have limited resources. Can't she see how wrong this is? The children are suffering too.' She thought of poor Loretta and her baby that never lived to see the light of day, and anger surged through her.

'Her hate has blinded her to the suffering of the people. I never thought I'd see the day when the Innocenti turned their backs on the villagers, but unfortunately that day has arrived.'

'I should go to talk to her, make her see sense.'

'No!' Rosa gripped Sara's arm tightly. 'You must stay away from the villa. Promise me you won't go anywhere near there. It's too dangerous.'

'Why?' Sara pulled her arm out of Rosa's grip and rubbed it.

Rosa gathered her skirts and stood, hooking the basket over her arm. 'I have to go, your mother will be suspicious otherwise.' She gave Sara a quick hug, then stepped back, brushing a tear from her eye. 'I don't know how all this will end, but there is much unrest in the village and if things don't improve...' She sniffed loudly. 'For once in your life, take heed of what I tell you, and stay away.'

Sara watched, stunned, as Rosa turned and fled across the cemetery. She saw her slow down near the statue of an angel and press her hand against its bowed head, then she hurried through the gate and was gone.

Anna-Maria listened in silence as Sara told her everything Rosa had said. They sat in the old woman's kitchen drinking tea, the tap-tap-tapping of the Hanging Tree barely noticeable.

'What did she mean, that I was to stay away from the villa?' Sara asked. 'Have you heard anything in the village?'

'I hear much and say little, that is how I have survived all these years,' Anna-Maria replied with a frown. 'Although my dreams are still haunted by what I saw the night of the storm.'

'What did you see? You never spoke again of it.'

Anna-Maria pulled her shawl around her, shivering slightly. 'There are some souls that never leave the tree, just like Bob will never leave his resting place down by the river. They are there to help the other souls, and to guide me and anyone else who asks for guidance. All I know is that something bad is going to happen, and that the villa is at the centre of the darkness surrounding us. Two years ago it was only a vague sensation, now it is becoming stronger day by day. The wheels are turning and no one can stop them. It will happen, come what may. Our lives will never be the same again, for better or for worse.'

Sara felt the hairs lifting on the nape of her neck. 'What's going to happen?' she whispered, her voice trembling.

'Do you really want to know? Even if this knowledge comes at a price?'

Sara nodded, her mouth dry.

'Come then.' Anna-Maria led her out of the cottage to the Hanging Tree. She gestured to Sara to stand beside her, beneath the lowest branch. 'Close your eyes and let the images come. Don't open them until I tell you to.'

Sara closed her eyes. A leaf brushed against her head, as soft as a mother's fingers caressing her baby's cheek. Anna-Maria chanted in a strange tongue, the melody falling and rising as if carried by the wind. It wrapped itself around them, tendrils stroking their hair, their bare arms, their ankles, as the breeze blew more strongly, carrying the old woman's song.

From the darkness behind her eyelids, Sara saw an image of flickering lights, orange and red, dancing over the horizon. A fierce wind blew across the land, bending the flames before it, stirring up clouds of smoke. She heard voices shouting angrily, bodiless in the hazy twilight, getting louder as they approached. She desperately wanted to open her eyes, but Anna-Maria had told her not to. Fear gripped her as the voices got closer, the wind blowing the flames over her, searing her skin with their heat...

She couldn't bear it any longer. She opened her eyes, gasping for breath, and screamed at the sight of two corpses dangling from the branch in front of her. The world went dark as she mercifully fainted.

✒

'Sara. Sara!' Anna-Maria's voice came from far away, penetrating the fog in her head. Several drops of water fell on her face, and she reached out with her tongue to catch them. 'Sara, wake up.' Anna-Maria's voice was more urgent, closer.

With an effort, Sara opened her eyes. 'Water,' she pleaded, her voice hoarse.

'Here.'

Drops of water fell on her mouth and she drank them thirstily.

'Lie still for a moment, until you gather your wits again. You fainted, child.'

Sara took several deep breaths, her head slowly clearing.

'What did you see?' The old woman's hand trembled as she stroked Sara's hair and wiped a damp cloth over her face.

Sara sat up, her head spinning. She took hold of Anna-Maria to steady herself. 'Bodies,' she whispered, looking up at the branch of the Hanging Tree above them. 'Two bodies.' She burst into tears, and the old woman hugged her to her bosom until she calmed down.

'The souls have shown us what will be, but not when or how. We must be patient and wait until all is revealed to us.'

'Can we change what is to happen?' Sara asked, wiping her nose on the sleeve of her dress.

'No. Once they have shown us, it must be so. The wheel of time cannot be stopped.'

Sara burst into tears again, the image of her parents hanging from the tree burned into her mind.

19

Groups of men stood huddled in the streets, talking in hushed voices and gesticulating angrily. Sara gripped the basket in her hand, and nodded a brief hello as she passed them. Most smiled back at her; others stood, lips pursed, until she'd passed, then broke out into whispered rants again.

She could feel the tension in the air, so dense she could have sliced it with a knife. She'd heard that more labourers from the coast had arrived up at the estate, working the land the villagers had once cared for, and she could hardly blame the locals for getting riled.

She went from cottage to cottage, treating the first coughs and colds of the season, verrucas, cuts, and a broken finger, too busy to think about the unrest all around her. Her patients were mainly the elderly, too frail to walk up to the cottage, and they treated her kindly.

'So, young lady, when is you thinking of getting yerself a husband, then?' Signora Pacini asked her with a cackle, nudging her in the ribs with her bony elbow.

'Now, Mamma, that's enough.' Ada, her daughter, sighed.

'She's got enough on her plate looking after you, without you asking questions like that!'

Sara laughed. 'Ada's right. Now sit still; I'm going to rub some of this unguent on your back, that'll help shift the phlegm so you can breathe better.' She rubbed vigorously, the sweet perfume of the herbs filling the room.

'She insisted on staying outside the other night, even though it was windy,' Ada scolded. 'I told her it weren't good for her, but she wouldn't listen. Now look at her.'

Signora Pacini chuckled, then started coughing. Sara waited until she'd coughed up a large ball of green phlegm, which she spat into the fire.

'Ooh, that feels better,' she said, sighing heavily.

'I'm glad to hear it.' Sara turned to Ada. 'I'll leave you the unguent. Rub it on three times a day, and help her get rid of the catarrh whenever she can. Keep her indoors, wrapped up warm, and I'll come back in a couple of days to see how she is.'

'Did you hear that, Mamma? No more going outside for a while, eh?' Ada patted the old woman's arm affectionately, the worry on her face belying her harsh tone. 'I swear she'll be the death of me,' she said as Sara picked up her things and got ready to leave. 'Tell me, what do I owe you?'

'Nothing,' Sara said. The women's ramshackle cottage was sparsely furnished, the shutters hanging from their hinges. Bernardo had told her that Ada's husband had gone down to the valley to look for work some months before, leaving Ada to care for her elderly mother alone. The two barely survived on what Ada managed to grow in their garden and the scrawny chickens Sara had seen scratching in the dirt when she arrived. She dreaded to think how the women would cope during the long, harsh winter.

Ada glared at her. 'We aren't a charity case,' she said haughtily. 'We pays our way. Now, what do I owe you.'

'For the moment, nothing.' Ada opened her mouth to speak, but Sara held up her hand. 'When I've finished treating your mother, I'll let you know. All right?'

Ada nodded, and Sara saw the flash of relief cross her face.

'The most important thing is to get your mother well again. If you do as I said, she'll be better in no time.' Sara rummaged around in her basket and pulled out a small cotton bag. 'Make her some tea using these herbs, get her to drink three or four cups a day. It will help shift the catarrh too.'

'Thank you, Sara.' Ada took the bag, then reached over and kissed her on both cheeks. 'Mamma always spoke highly of your grandmother, said there never was a better healer. I'm glad you've taken over the reins, so to speak, we was desperate for a healer here in the village.'

'I'm glad too, and I hope I can be half the healer she was. She was a great woman, I'm honoured to follow in her footsteps.' Sara waved goodbye as she unlatched the rickety gate. 'Remember to keep her warm,' she called.

'Don't worry, I'll make sure she does as she's told,' Ada called back, laughing as she returned indoors.

Signora Pacini was her last patient of the morning, and with a sigh of relief, Sara headed back towards the village square. As she rounded the corner, she saw a mass of people pushing each other and yelling. She stopped, undecided as to what to do, then caught a glimpse of Bernardo in the middle of them, his nose bleeding as he shouted incomprehensible words. She ran over, bottles clinking as her basket swayed to and fro, and shoved her way through the crowd.

'What's going on?' she shouted, her worry for Bernardo overcoming her fear of so many people crowding around, all with hatred on their faces.

'Sara! Go home,' Bernardo ordered, panting heavily as he

looked at the wall of people surrounding him, holding his fists up, ready to punch someone.

Sara grabbed hold of a woman near her. 'Please, tell me what's happening.'

'He was talking with Oliviero and his friends, then all of a sudden they started fighting,' the young woman said, her face flushed with excitement.

'But why?'

'I'll tell you why.' A short, stocky man with a bull neck pushed his way over to her, his meaty hands shoving people aside. He ignored their complaints as he stood in front of her, legs apart, hands folded across his chest. 'Him, that *servant*, telling us not to bother with them up at the villa, they're not worth the trouble.' He spat on the ground, near Sara's feet. 'Not worth the trouble? They's caused the trouble, hiring in foreigners, usin' them machines instead of us hard-working labourers. We've worked the land for years, us and our fathers and their fathers before them, and now they've thrown us away like useless objects. We can't even go on strike without them callin' the police. Do you know how many of us got beaten up the other week? Poor Carlo ended up with a cracked skull!'

Sara shook her head, confused; she hadn't heard about any strike. She realised how isolated she was at the cottage, away from the troubles in the village, and was upset with Bernardo for not telling her.

'We're not standin' for it anymore! And you and the stable boy had better not interfere, if you knows what's good for you.' He turned and glared at Bernardo. 'Get goin', before I change my mind and hits you again.'

He shoved Bernardo towards Sara, the crowd parting to let him through. Bernardo stomped away, ignoring Sara, who had to run to keep up with him. He remained silent until they reached the dirt track that led to the cottage, then he slammed his fist into the nearest tree.

'Bloody idiots!' he shouted, startling a cloud of blackbirds. They rose up into the sky, squawking at the intruders.

Sara ran over, but he waved her away. 'What happened? Why did they hit you?'

He groaned. 'Because I tried to convince them that violence wasn't the way. Anna-Maria was right, or at least her spirits were.'

'I-I don't understand.'

'They wouldn't listen, and who can blame them? They can't take any more. It's not just the machines, it's the fact the Innocenti are hiring labourers from afar. They said no one will listen to them so they're going to make your parents pay, and soon.'

Sara knocked at the servants' door, glancing around nervously in case anyone had seen her. She'd approached the villa from the woods and run across the open patch of grass, praying no one was looking out of the windows.

Rosa opened the door and shrieked when she saw her. 'What are you doing here?'

'Shush, Rosa, let me in,' Sara begged. Rosa stepped back and Sara went into the kitchen.

'You'll have me whipped if they find out,' Rosa whispered. The kitchen was empty, except for an ancient cat, who flicked its shredded ears and went back to sleep again.

'I'm sorry, but I had to come,' Sara said quietly, her voice urgent. 'There's trouble down in the village–'

'I know, I see it every day, remember?' Rosa interrupted her.

'Not like this. Bernardo and I were there today. Bernardo was in a fight.'

'What?'

Sara nodded grimly. 'I found him in the middle of a group of men, and they were beating him because he dared to speak against them. The villagers are planning to do something to my parents. They're starving down there, Rosa, they can't take any more. We don't know what they're going to do, but it won't be pleasant. You must tell my parents to leave.'

'Leave? They'll never leave here. They'll see it as the coward's way out.'

'Go travelling, then.' Sara was exasperated. 'They have to go away from the house, today. We've no idea when the villagers are going to come, but they will come. Please say you'll speak to them. You're the only one they'll listen to.'

'I'll try.' Rosa's voice was full of doubt. 'They do what they want, you know that, and they won't let themselves be terrorised by a handful of locals.'

'I've got a feeling it'll be more than a handful,' Sara said. She pushed the images she'd seen at the Hanging Tree firmly to the back of her mind.

'Why do you want to help them? If you don't mind me asking. After everything they've done to you.'

'They're my parents.' Sara's shoulders slumped. 'I can't just stand back and watch.'

Rosa hugged her. 'I'll talk to them, I promise, but I can't say that they'll listen.'

'Thank you. I can't ask you to do more than that,' Sara replied, hugging her back. 'And take care of yourself. The first sign of trouble, get out of here.'

'Don't worry, I will.' Rosa made the sign of the cross. 'These are dark times, Lady Sara. God willing, we all live through them.'

20

Sara woke with a start, suddenly alert. A thin layer of sweat coated her skin, and she felt as if she was suffocating. She sat up, trying to calm her breathing, her eyes slowly growing accustomed to the dark room. A faint glimmer came from the far corner, a shimmering light that faded and brightened as she watched. She swung her legs over the edge of the bed, to go and open the shutters.

'Don't.' The voice was inside her head but also about her, echoing around the room.

'Why?' She peered into the gloom, her eyes making out the shadowy forms of furniture before resting again on the glimmering light.

'I don't have much time,' the voice whispered. It seemed to come from a trickle of dust motes caught in a moonbeam that filtered through the shutters.

'Who are you?' Sara sat with her back against the headboard, clutching the sheets to her body.

'Stay in the cottage. No matter what you hear or see, stay inside. And Bernardo too, he mustn't go either.' The voice became stronger all of a sudden, and Sara recognised it. 'But he will, I know him too well. Tell him I look forward to being with him once more, dearest Sara.'

'Nonna? What do you mean by that? Is he going to die?' Sara gasped, her throat constricting with terror.

The light faded, the shimmering so faint that Sara could barely make it out anymore. She stared at the corner, willing it to return, certain that it had been her grandmother, but there was only darkness. She waited for a while, thoughts racing round her head. When the light didn't reappear she lay back down, but sleep eluded her as she went over her grandmother's words.

The sound of angry voices disturbed the stillness of the night. She leaped out of bed, grabbing her dressing gown and wrapping it tightly around her before opening the shutters. The sight of flickering torches far off in the distance among the trees brought back the memory of the vision she'd seen.

'Dear lord, they're going up to the villa!' She flung her gown and nightdress on the floor and quickly pulled on an old gardening smock, then ran downstairs.

Bernardo was by the back door, pulling on his boots.

'Nonno, what's going on?'

'Sara, go to bed.' His face was pale in the moonlight, his grey hair standing on end.

'How can I? It's the villagers, isn't it? They're going to the villa for my parents!'

He caught hold of her shoulders and held her close. 'You have to be strong, Sara. I've no idea what they've got in mind, but I'm going to see what they're up to. Maybe I can help in some way. But you've got to stay here!'

'No, you can't!' The voice echoed around her head, her dead grandmother's voice, telling her that Bernardo would die.

'Don't talk nonsense, Sara. I have to help if I can.'

She shook her head. 'You don't understand! Nonna came to me while I was sleeping. She said we weren't to go to the villa.'

Bernardo paled. 'Gi-Ginevra. Are you sure?'

'Yes.' Sara put her hand on his cheek, the stubble rasping against her fingers. 'She appeared in my room and woke me. She sounded desperate. She insisted we mustn't leave the cottage.'

Bernardo sighed and patted her arm. 'It was only a dream, Sara. The mind plays funny tricks on us, especially when we are asleep. So many times I think I've seen her.' He shrugged. 'I'm sorry, I can't sit indoors like a coward when God knows what is happening up at the villa. I have to go. Pray that you were dreaming and wait for me to return.'

Sara wriggled out of his grasp and quickly slipped on her boots. 'Do you really think I'm going to sit here and wait for you to come home? If you must go, even after my warning, I'm coming with you to stop you from doing anything stupid.'

He opened his mouth to say something, but they could hear more shouting and cries in the distance. 'You're as stubborn as your grandmother! Come then, but be quiet and stay behind me.'

Sara followed him out of the cottage, ignoring the uneasy feeling in her heart.

The voices grew louder as they cut through the woods towards the villa. They could see the torches bobbing up and down as the crowd made its way up the driveway, finally stopping before the enormous front door.

'How many people!' Sara gasped. It seemed as if most of the village was there, men, women and even some children, all caught up in a maelstrom of anger as they shouted over one another.

Bernardo turned and placed his finger on his lips. 'Shh,' he warned. 'Let's try to get closer, but stay in the shelter of the trees. If they should see us...'

He didn't need to say any more. Sara could see that the mob's blood was up, and in their rage they would turn on anyone who appeared to be their enemy. They crept closer, until they reached the last of the trees. Bernardo gestured to stop, and they crouched behind the trunks.

She watched, shocked, as a villager tossed a rock through one of the downstairs windows. At the sound of glass smashing, the crowd let loose a mighty cheer. As if it had been a signal, others threw more rocks, everyone becoming more frenzied as the windows caved in.

Then the first torch was thrown through one of the broken windows. Sara suppressed a scream as hungry orange flames flickered in the dark night, feeding on the heavy velvet curtains. Bernardo gripped her hand as the crowd surged forward and threw more torches. They could see movement behind the upstairs windows as servants woke up and looked out, then there was screaming and shouting from inside.

'The villa won't burn, will it?' Sara asked Bernardo, her jaw aching from where she'd been clenching it so tightly.

'Not the floor or walls, they're made of stone, but the ceilings, the furniture, the tapestries on the walls, the curtains all will. They've got to get out of there!' Bernardo replied, his voice urgent.

The front door was suddenly flung open and Sara watched, horrified, as her parents stood side by side in the entrance. They said something, but their voices were drowned out by the sound of the crowd jeering at them.

Her father held up his hands, trying to quell the shouting, but to no avail. He straightened his shoulders, feet apart, head held high, a stance Sara had seen countless times while growing up that had never failed to make her tremble. His face was set in a stern expression as he glared at the people before him. The shouting gradually ceased, falling to a constant murmur.

'Your troubles are known to me, and I appreciate your concerns,' he said, his voice loud and clear. 'Come back in the morning, and we shall discuss matters.'

Someone in the crowd spat at him.

He took a handkerchief out of his pocket and wiped his face, his cheeks flushed red. 'Begone, good for nothing rabble!' he shouted, his eyes wide with fury.

Like a terrible, demonic creature, the people surged forward and grabbed hold of the conte and contessa. Lucrezia screamed as they grabbed her hair, her arms, her body, ripping her clothes in their frenzied attack, and writhed to get away from their clutching hands. Her husband struck out, catching one a glancing blow on the cheek, before being overwhelmed. His body sagged as a villager hit him on the back of the head with a heavy stick, the sickening crunch audible from where Sara and Bernardo were watching in shocked silence. Lucrezia stopped struggling. The crowd cheered as several men hoisted the conte and contessa into the air, holding their prey high above their heads. A shout rang out, and the crowd strode away from the villa.

'No!' Sara screamed, leaping to her feet.

'Stay here, Sara, you can't do anything.' Bernardo grabbed her waist and held her tightly to him.

'Where are they taking them?' she sobbed, struggling to get free.

'To the village, it would seem,' he said grimly as the crowd went back down the driveway, a tidal wave that would crush anything in its path.

'The Hanging Tree,' Sara moaned. 'They're taking them to the tree. I have to do something.'

Bernardo shook her roughly. 'You can't do anything, don't you understand? If they see you, they'll hang you too.'

'I can't leave them! Even after everything they've done, they're still my parents.'

Terrified cries from the villa interrupted them. They looked up to see a group of servants at one of the upstairs windows, shouting and screaming in fear. Wherever they looked, flames burned brightly on the ground floor.

'Rosa's up there!' Bernardo shouted, pointing. 'I have to help!' He ran across to the courtyard, where other servants, and a few villagers who had remained behind, had formed a line from the pond to the villa to throw buckets of water over the fire. Sara was close behind him.

'You'll never put the flames out,' he snapped. 'Get inside and help those who are trapped.'

They turned and looked at him, their faces black with soot. 'We already tried, and we're not going back in there,' one man said. The others nodded in agreement.

Bernardo grunted in frustration, then ripped the sleeve off his shirt, dipped it in a bucket of water, and tied it around his face so it covered his mouth and nose.

'You can't go in there!' Sara grabbed his arm, but he shook her off.

'I need to save them,' he said, his voice muffled underneath the cloth. 'You stay here, promise me you won't go after your parents.'

'I can't,' Sara sobbed, torn. 'I have to know what happens to them.' She broke away and ran across the garden towards the drive.

'Sara!' she heard from behind her, but she closed her ears and her heart, and fled in the footsteps of the mob.

'Promise me you'll stay back,' Sara heard Bernardo call, his voice fading as she continued her flight along the drive. 'Please come back to me, I can't lose you as well.' The screams from the villa became louder as the flames roared and crackled behind them.

Sara looked back once, to see Bernardo charging into the burning building. Tears streamed down her cheeks as she wondered if she would ever see him again, her grandmother's words still ringing in her ears.

21

Crouched behind a bush, Sara could see the villagers stood beneath the Hanging Tree. She recognised Oliviero, the short, stocky man who had hit Bernardo the day before, standing in front of her parents. He raised his arms to the sky and tilted his head back, eyes closed, and recited a prayer. The crowd was silent, anticipation running through it like a static charge from lightning.

Oliviero reached the end of his prayer and lowered his arms by his side. He looked at the conte and contessa, a grim expression on his face, then turned to the crowd. His voice rang loud and clear as he spoke.

'We have before us the Conte and Contessa di Gallicano.' There were shouts and jeers, people jostled each other, and someone shouted, 'Bastards', before things settled down again. He spoke, nodding at the villagers. 'I know. We are all suffering here, while these *maiali* continue to ignore our plight, hiring worthless labourers from afar to work the land – work we was born to do. We must listen to our children cry because they's hungry, while we ourselves haven't eaten for days. We must bury our dead, while we barely have the strength to dig their graves.

Mothers weep for their babes, husbands for their wives who die giving birth, and children are left to fend for theirselves, orphaned. And we know who is to blame, don't we?'

An angry roar burst forth from the crowd, low at first, but quickly rising in volume. A chant rose in the air, 'Pigs, pigs, pigs, pigs', over and over again, echoing through the branches of the tree. Those holding sticks thumped them on the ground, others stomped their feet, and they all raised a clenched fist to the sky.

The conte and contessa stood immobile, their faces pale in the gloom. Their clothes were ripped in places, and the contessa's immaculate hair was knotted and dishevelled. Sara could see her mother's lips moving, and wondered if she was saying a prayer or calling on the healers to save her. For the first time since Sara could remember, she saw fear on the contessa's face. Her father wavered, appearing to almost collapse, then recovered himself at the last moment. His eyes anxiously scanned the crowd, and Sara huddled further into the shadows, terrified. She couldn't do anything to save them, it was likely the crowd would rip her to pieces as well, but she was ashamed of her cowardice.

Oliviero spoke again. 'We, the people of Gallicano, are tired of being treated worse than animals by these so-called noblemen and women. We only asked to be allowed to have some dignity, to earn enough to feed our families, but we were denied even that. Therefore, we have decided to take matters into our own hands. These two before us have sullied the name of the Innocenti family, long-time benefactors of our valley, casting us aside as worthless and bringing in others to do the work we were born to do. But no longer!' His voice rose to a shout, and the crowd cheered. 'Now it is our time to take back our dignity, our livelihood, our right to work this land, by consigning their souls to the Hanging Tree!' He tilted his chin at a group of men standing beside him. 'Take them.'

He pointed at the conte and contessa.

While four of the men grabbed her parents by the arms, others threw two ropes over the ancient branch. Sara shuddered at the sight of the empty nooses swinging beneath the tree. A surge of excitement ran through the crowd as Oliviero placed the nooses around her parents' necks and the ropes were pulled taut. Two men led a pair of horses through the crowd, coming to a stop before them. Despite their struggling, the others hoisted her parents onto the horses' backs as if they were sacks of flour, and the two men quieted the animals as the crowd whistled and shouted.

'We will no longer tolerate injustice, we will no longer bow to our capitalist masters who try to break us and then discard us,' Oliviero declared. A hush came over the crowd, the air thick with anticipation. The conte twisted his body, despair on his face, while the contessa sat straight and still, gazing into the distance.

There was a moment of utter silence, where time came to a halt, and infinite possibilities lay before everyone gathered there. Nothing moved, no one breathed, there was no sound, even the light seemed to have been sucked from the stars above. Death lingered nearby, waiting, eager.

Then Oliviero nodded to the men holding the horses, and time began once more. A horse whinnied. The branch creaked as the men holding the ropes leaned back, bracing themselves.

Hoof beats. Heartbeats. Seconds turned into eons. The night breeze passed through the branches of the tree, the leaves whispering long-kept secrets in its ear.

Two dull thuds filled the air.

Sara turned her face away as a great cheer went up from the crowd. She sank to the ground, her body wracked by heaving sobs. Death had come to collect its debt; what had happened beneath the Hanging Tree had already been decided a long time before. She wept for her parents' stubbornness, and she wept for the villagers, unable to bear the situation any longer. And she wept for the curse, once again devastating her family. She pressed her cheek against the ground, the cool, damp grass bringing relief, and gave vent to her grief.

❦

Some time later, she felt the ground vibrating as the crowd passed by, their steps slower and heavier now that the excitement was over. She wiped away her tears and slowly got up, then stepped out from behind the bush, not caring what they would do if they saw her. Oliviero stopped before her and removed his hat.

'I'm sorry you had to see that,' he said, his voice soft. 'We wish you no harm, you are a healer. A true Innocenti.' He bowed to her, replaced his hat, and joined the rest of the villagers as they traipsed back to their homes.

Sara watched them pass, but no one else looked her way. She waited until the last had left, then turned to the Hanging Tree and Anna-Maria's cottage. The old woman was there, her arms raised towards the bodies swinging gently in the night air, her keening melody rising up into the branches of the tree.

She glanced at Sara as she approached, nodding in approval, and continued her song. Sara stood next to her, the hair on her arms rising as she forced herself to look upon her parents' faces for the last time. She felt that she owed them that much, even though she knew the grotesque image would haunt her dreams for the rest of her life.

The song stopped. 'Will you help me finish the rite?'

Sara hesitated. 'What do I have to do?'

'I'll show you.' Anna-Maria took hold of her hand. 'Don't fret. 'Tis a wondrous thing to see.'

Sara sniffed.

'Do as I do, it will all be over soon.' The old woman chanted, ancient words that flowed into Sara's veins, through her body, all the way to her heart. She joined in the best she could, and together they caught her parents' souls, sending them on their way.

Sara looked up at the two bodies, aware that they were mere empty shells. The essence that had been her parents had gone, carried away on the breeze by the soul catcher's song. She reached out and touched the trunk of the tree, its bark rough beneath her fingertips, and took long, deep breaths, trying to find some calm amidst the storm in her head.

'Now you must go back to the villa, there are people there who need your help,' Anna-Maria said gently, passing her a basket filled with remedies and bandages. 'The dead will take care of their own here.'

Sara stumbled away, her head and heart swirling with emotion. Somehow she made her way through the woods, back to the villa and the destruction. The whole area was lit up as bright as day by the fire still raging inside. There was utter confusion; some people stood, shouting and yelling, their bodies silhouetted against the fire, while others lay slumped, groaning in their agony. A few were motionless, and she knew they would never move again. She waited a moment longer, reluctant to leave the shadows beneath the trees, then straightened her shoulders and stepped into the mayhem.

She moved among the people lying on the grass and tended to their burns and wounds, trying to calm their anguish, her own emotions numb as she worked steadily through the night. Whenever she had a moment she searched desperately for Bernardo and Rosa, but couldn't find them anywhere.

She finished treating the last person as dawn broke, and

stood up to stretch, her muscles protesting after the long hours of tending to patients.

'Go home, Lady Sara.' Duccio, one of the gardeners, appeared before her, his face grimy with sweat and soot. 'You can't do any more here.'

'Bernardo?'

He shook his head. 'I haven't seen him.'

Sara picked up her basket and made her way back through the woods. No birds twittered, no insects were out on their early morning business. There was a deathly hush all around, as though every living being was in mourning for what had taken place that night. Her limbs heavy with exhaustion and grief, she hurried home as fast as she could.

As she walked across the clearing towards the cottage, the dragonfly appeared and hovered around her head. Dreading what she would find, she opened the back door and went inside.

22

Rosa raised her head wearily from the kitchen table, her bloodshot eyes wide in her soot-covered face.

'Rosa!' Sara rushed over and hugged her. 'You're safe, thank goodness! Where's Nonno?'

'Over there.' Rosa's voice was croaky from the smoke, but Sara could see that she seemed to be breathing well. She looked over to the corner where Rosa had pointed, and saw a form lying on a pallet in the shadows. 'He insisted we carry him here. I got the others to set up a bed for him so he'd be comfortable. I gave him some water and I've been waiting for you to come back.'

Sara went over to him and knelt beside the pallet. 'Nonno,' she whispered.

He opened his eyes and raised his blackened hand towards her. She winced at his burns, the skin red raw beneath the dirt and soot.

'Don't talk, Nonno, it's all right. Just rest,' she said, stroking his hair. His breathing made a rattling noise in his chest and his face was contorted with pain.

'The chest,' he said hoarsely. 'Rosa has the chest, and the book.' He closed his eyes again, the effort of speaking too much.

'Is that true?' Sara leaped to her feet.

Rosa picked up a small wooden chest from the floor and put it on the table. 'Your mother gave it to me before–' She wiped away a tear. 'Before she went down to face the villagers.'

'My mother?' Sara said, shocked.

'She told me she couldn't let it burn with the villa, that I had to get it to you, whatever happened. She said…' Rosa gulped, overcome with emotion. 'She said to tell you she was sorry, that she gives you her blessing, even though she understands you may not want it.' She blew her nose. 'Your mother knew what would happen if she went outside, but she did it anyway. She had her faults, but she sacrificed herself to save the rest of us, otherwise we would all have burned in there. Somewhere, deep inside, she had some Innocenti blood in her after all.'

Sara pushed back the tears. She was tired and emotional, but she still had work to do. Her grandfather was suffering, and she had to help him. She looked down at the chest, briefly admiring the dragonfly carved on the top, then opened it. The book was there, its dark leather binding scratched and worn, the pages yellow with age, the thin strip of leather tied around it frayed. She lifted it out of the chest and gazed at it with reverence.

'After so long,' she said softly. A cough and a groan from the corner brought her back to the present. 'Right. Rosa, take some chamomile from the pantry, boil some water, and make compresses for the burns. And get some of the lavender oil I prepared, that will soothe the pain while we're waiting for the chamomile.'

Rosa rushed off to the pantry, while Sara took the book and a candle over to Bernardo's pallet and sat down next to him.

'Don't worry, Nonno, we'll soon have you better,' she said, flicking through the pages.

He reached out and grabbed her arm. 'No, Sara.' He coughed. 'It's my time, I can feel it. Leave me be.'

Tears pricked at Sara's eyes. 'I can make you better,' she insisted, hearing the doubt in her own voice and hating herself for it. His hand gripped her even more tightly.

'You know I'm right,' he mumbled. 'Ginevra told you, didn't she? That's why you didn't want me to go to the villa. It wasn't a dream after all.'

She looked at his burned face and hands, and listened to him struggling to breathe, and knew he was dying.

'I can't do nothing.'

'Stubborn as ever,' Bernardo whispered, his laugh turning to a hacking cough.

'I'm an Innocenti, remember?' Sara replied, tears filling her eyes.

Rosa came over with the lavender oil and some clean cloths. Sara took them from her, then turned her attention back to her grandfather, her expert eyes seeking out the worst of his injuries.

'What happened up at the villa? Did Nonno get you out?' She spoke without looking at Rosa, and continued to examine her grandfather's wounds.

'He came charging up the stairs, like a knight without his steed, and got us all out on the roof. The others managed to slide down a rope and get to safety, but I had the chest. I couldn't do it.' Rosa stroked Bernardo's wispy hair, tears falling down her cheeks. 'The old fool said he'd carry me over his shoulder, and wrapped me in a sheet. He took the cloth off his face and tied it around mine. He said it would help me breathe through all the smoke.'

'Told you it'd work, didn't I?' he croaked. Sara shushed him, and gently washed the grime off his hands with the oil.

'He carried the chest, with me over his shoulder, down the stairs, through the flames and out the servants' door. I've no idea how he did it, I was almost passing out with fear.'

'Oh, Nonno,' Sara said, her heart full of pride and despair. She dabbed some oil on a clean piece of cloth and placed it on a nasty burn on his face.

'Steady, Sara,' he whimpered.

'Sorry. Rosa, the chamomile?'

'Yes, I'll do it right away.' She bustled over to the stove, pots clattering as she hurried to put some water on to boil.

'Nonno, I'm sorry for the things I said when I found out about you and my grandmother,' Sara said. 'I can't believe I was so horrible.'

'It's all right, Sara, I understand what a shock it must have been. I've watched you grow up, right from when you were born. I taught you to ride and look after the horses, and I saw you become the young woman your grandmother wanted you to be.' He lay gasping after such a long speech, and Sara gently brushed his mouth with a damp cloth.

'I'll carry those memories in my heart,' she said quietly. 'I wish I'd known you were my grandfather.'

'I think, deep down, you did.'

Sara smiled. 'You may be right.' She panicked as his breathing became a harsh, rasping sound.

'It hurts to breathe, Sara.' Bernardo placed a hand on his chest. 'Right here.'

'I can't find anything in the book,' Sara said, turning the pages. 'There must be something, but I need more time.' Tears rolled down her cheeks.

A shadow fell over her hand. Sara raised her head. The shadowy figure she'd seen the night before in her bedroom was standing there, the outline stronger now.

'Sara, I've come for Bernardo. I will look after him, don't worry.'

'Grandmother?'

'Ginevra?' Bernardo was staring at the shadow standing over him, his eyes wide open.

The shadow leaned over and stroked his forehead, its touch seeming to soothe the old man's pain. Sara watched as her grandmother placed her lips on Bernardo's mouth and drew his breath into her. His chest rose once, twice, then no more. Her grandmother stood up straight, and another shadow joined her, twinkling in the candlelight. Sara saw her grandfather as he must have been all those years ago, a strong, robust youth in the prime of his life. He turned towards her, as if to say something, and then they were gone.

The two women covered his body with a sheet, their hearts heavy with grief.

'We need to call the priest,' Rosa said, sniffling.

'You look like you're about to collapse at any moment, and I don't feel much better,' Sara said. 'We'll get a few hours' sleep first. You take my bed, I'll stay down here in case anyone calls round. There'll be more injured people to tend to today.'

Rosa hesitated. 'I'm sorry about your parents, Sara. I know they had their faults – I know that better than anyone – but they didn't deserve to die like that.'

'Thank you.' Sara didn't know what else to say. She had no more energy left, and her head was filled with a murky fog.

Rosa sighed. 'I'll let you get some rest. Things will be easier after a good sleep.'

Sara looked at her grandfather's body underneath the sheet, and wondered how she would ever be able to go on.

23

Rosa left in the afternoon for the village. She returned with several men and a horse and cart. Sara stood on the back doorstep, her arms folded across her chest.

'Lady Sara, we're sorry for your loss. Bernardo was a good man, one of the best.'

Sara pursed her lips and stared at the men before her, afraid to speak in case she started screeching like a fishwife at them for what they had done.

'We've come to take him to the church, so he can be buried proper. The priest is waiting.'

She stood aside and gestured to the men to enter. They took off their hats and filed inside in silence.

A few minutes later, they came back out, carrying Bernardo on his pallet. They carefully placed him in the back of the cart, and gathered around, heads bowed.

Rosa took hold of Sara's hand. 'Let's go.'

The small group solemnly made its way through the woods to the road, the creaking of the horse's leather and the cart's wheels the only sound to be heard.

Others joined the procession as they reached the village,

until a long line of people followed the cart up through the winding streets to the church at the top. The priest was standing by the iron gates, his black robes billowing around his legs in the breeze. He greeted Sara with a firm shake of the hand, and patted her shoulder as he offered his condolences.

'These are terrible times,' he told her. 'The sinners shall be punished, and people like Bernardo will be rewarded when God receives them in Heaven.'

Sara pushed back an angry retort. *You can punish the sinners all you want, but Bernardo will still be dead*, she wanted to shout. *And what about my parents? Did they deserve to die like that? Will you be holding a funeral for them too?* Instead she kept quiet, pressing her handkerchief over her nose to avoid having to reply. He nodded understandingly and guided her across the cemetery to the newly dug grave. There was already a large crowd of people gathered around, waiting for the service to begin.

The ceremony was mercifully brief, the priest's sombre tones carrying across the graveyard to the people stood further away. The local undertaker, Signor Martinelli, had been waiting with a coffin, which four of the villagers were lowering into the ground. Sara could hear the women of the village sniffing and snuffling, some blowing their noses loudly, and hated them for their hypocrisy. Many of them had been at the villa the night before, throwing their torches through the broken windows, determined to burn it to the ground, along with all those inside.

As soon as the final prayer had been said, she turned and walked away before anyone could stop and speak to her. She couldn't bear it, not today. She hadn't said a word since she'd left the cottage, her heart too full of grief.

Rosa caught up with her, panting slightly. 'Lady Sara, wait.'

Sara continued on her way.

'Lady Sara, please.'

Sara stopped and slowly turned to face the servant-woman. She'd never seen her look so old; deep wrinkles had appeared around her eyes and on her forehead overnight, aging her at least ten years. Rosa held out her arms, and Sara fell into her embrace.

'What am I going to do now, Rosa?' Sara sobbed. 'How can I carry on alone?' She was filled with dread at the thought of how empty her life would be from now on.

'You won't be alone, Lady Sara,' Rosa said, hugging her tightly. 'I won't leave your side. If you'll have me, that is.'

'Thank you, Rosa,' Sara replied with a loud sniff. She pulled back from the woman's arms and wiped the tears from her face. 'But if you are to live at the cottage, you must stop calling me Lady Sara. It's just Sara. No more titles. From now on, the Innocenti are the same as anyone else from the village.'

'But–' Rosa frowned. 'You're the contessa now.'

'There'll be no more contessas, or lords, or ladies. Those titles died with my parents.'

'Lady Sara, you can't. This is your inheritance, your future. You're an Innocenti.'

'Exactly. I was born to be a healer, not a contessa. Either you accept this or you can find elsewhere to live. It's your choice.'

Rosa bowed her head. 'I understand. And I accept your wishes.'

Sara breathed a sigh of relief. She hadn't wanted to lose Rosa as well. 'Thank you. Now, before we return to the cottage, I'd like to go and see Anna-Maria.'

'Sara, I'm so sorry for everything that's happened.' The old woman's leathery face seemed even more wrinkled than usual, her usual sparkle gone.

'You foresaw it, Rosa tried to warn them,' Sara said, squeezing Anna-Maria's hand. Her heart felt heavy with grief at her loss. Too many people had died that night, thanks to her parents, although she knew the toll would have been much higher if her mother hadn't sacrificed herself at the end. 'They wouldn't listen.'

'They're in a better place now,' Anna-Maria reassured her. 'We helped their souls move on.'

'That's something, then, isn't it, Sara?' Rosa said.

An image of carrying out the ritual beneath the Hanging Tree with Anna-Maria flashed through Sara's mind, and she finally felt at peace. 'Yes. It helps to know they're safe now, wherever they are.' A thought struck her. 'What happened to their bodies?' She glanced up at the bough of the tree, bare of its undesirable fruit, as if the terrible events of the day before had never happened.

'Come. I'll show you.' Anna-Maria led them a little way down the path, to a rickety fence sagging beneath the weight of the straggling ivy growing over it. She opened a small gate and led them inside. Sara looked around at the mounds, each with a wooden cross at its head, and understood.

'You bury the victims of the Hanging Tree here, don't you?' she said, her voice low in respect for the dead before them.

'Only those who aren't claimed, or who can't be buried in a church cemetery.' Anna-Maria gestured to two freshly dug mounds. 'I thought you might prefer your parents to be buried here.'

'You buried them by yourself?' Rosa blurted out.

Sara gasped, horrified at the thought of the old woman digging the holes and dragging the bodies over to them.

'No, of course not. Some men from the village came this morning. They knew what they had to do. Don't worry.' Anna-Maria glanced over at Sara. 'They had nothing to do with this, they had the utmost respect for your parents.'

Sara nodded. 'You did the right thing. Maybe one day I'll move them to the family mausoleum, but for now they can rest in peace here. Thank you.'

'So, what will you do now?' Anna-Maria asked. 'Do you still want to be a healer, after everything that has happened?'

Sara had thought long and hard about it all morning. 'It's in my blood,' she said, spreading her hands wide. 'And now that I have the book–'

'You have the book?' Anna-Maria exclaimed.

'The contessa gave it to me and said to make sure Sara got it,' Rosa said, a hint of pride creeping into her voice.

Sara smiled. 'I'm sure you would like to see it, Anna-Maria.'

The old woman bustled them out of the burial ground, closing the gate behind her. 'I've only seen it a few times, up at the cottage. Your grandmother was very, let's say, possessive about it!'

'Come back to the cottage with us, we can look at it together. But I want to stop at the villa first.'

The three women looked at the ruined building. The stone had been discoloured by the fire, and black streaks covered the façade. The huge wooden doors were blackened and charred, and the acrid smell of smoke filled the air. Several servants were milling around, guarding some of the objects they'd managed to save when escaping the fire.

Duccio, the gardener Sara had spoken to only hours earlier, although it seemed like years, ran over to them.

'Lady Sara!'

'Have you been here all this time?' she asked.

'Me and the others thought it only right we stay here,' he said, yawning widely. 'We managed to put the fire out, though it's a disaster inside. It doesn't look too bad from here, but the rooms are ruined.' He coughed and spat black phlegm onto the grass.

'I want to go in and see for myself–'

'I wouldn't, Lady Sara,' he interrupted. 'It's not safe, the ceilings are falling in and there's debris everywhere. Young Roberto over there, he just made it out before the ceiling collapsed in the main hall.'

'I see. All right, tell everyone to go home and get some rest. It'll still be here tomorrow. And Duccio...' She took a deep breath. 'I'm no longer Lady Sara, if you would kindly remember. You and everyone else must call me Sara.'

A shocked look came over his face, but after a few seconds Duccio bowed his head, then ran off to the others.

Sara turned to Rosa and Anna-Maria. 'The villa will have to be torn down, I can't bear to look at it anymore. We'll live at the cottage, and forget it ever existed.'

'What about the servants? And the men who worked the land? All this started because they had nothing left, they were desperate.' Rosa shook her head. 'I don't want to justify what they did, nothing can do that, but tearing down the villa won't solve their problems.'

'I can't live there, Rosa, you must understand that. And with the house empty, the servants will have to find other employment. No, the villa must go.'

Anna-Maria and Rosa glanced at each other.

'A true healer belongs in the cottage,' Anna-Maria said.

Rosa nodded. 'Even though it breaks my heart to think of the villa being reduced to rubble, I agree,' she said sadly. 'But the land will still be yours, you'll need someone to work it.'

Sara's shoulders sagged, fearing their reaction to what she was about to say but determined to say it anyway. 'I've been awake all night, thinking this through,' she said slowly, trying to put her thoughts in order. 'I don't want to hear any arguments, I've already decided. The estate will be divided into plots, larger ones for the servants, the rest for the villagers who once worked here. Except for the ringleaders, they'll get nothing. If they have any sense, they'll leave the village. I want nothing more to do with this cursed land, and it should help settle the unrest. What do you think?' Despite her resolve, she suddenly needed their benediction.

Anna-Maria put her arm around Sara's shoulders. 'I think it's perfect,' she said quietly. 'Now, let's get away from this place before it blackens our souls as well.'

They sat around the kitchen table in the cottage, the book open before them.

'Now you can become a true healer,' Anna-Maria said, looking at Sara. 'Are you ready?'

'I believe so,' Sara replied, her heart hammering.

Anna-Maria pointed at the first page. 'Then add your name, child, and let's begin.'

24

NOVEMBER 1886

Having her grandmother's book meant Sara could finally become a true healer. Anna-Maria had pored over it, exclaiming in delight at the intricate drawings and handwritten recipes. The pantry was well stocked with dried herbs they'd gathered since Sara had been living at the cottage, and at long last they could make the remedies properly. Snug and warm inside, they worked all day long in the kitchen, the delicate aroma of sage, rosemary, and a myriad of other herbs drifting around them.

'We look like three witches around a cauldron,' Rosa remarked one evening.

Sara looked at the others, their faces sweating from standing over the wood-burning stove, stirring the enormous black pot full of boiling herbs, sleeves pushed back as far as they would go, their hair wild from the steam, and felt absurdly pleased at Rosa's comment.

'Isn't that what we are?' she said with a laugh. 'Good witches who honour the land we live on and the life the plants give us, but still witches with magical potions to make people well.'

'That may be so, but don't go around saying it!' Anna-Maria said, cackling.

Sara was grateful for the company of the two older women, she couldn't imagine how desolate her life would be without them. The death of her grandfather two years earlier had left a gaping hole in her heart, one she felt would never be filled. She often glanced at his armchair over by the fire, half expecting to see him sitting in it, puffing on his pipe, and the familiar ache would clutch at her insides.

He had been a part of her life ever since she was old enough to run down to the stables and watch him tend the horses, and he had always shown her kindness and patience. She missed his deep, gruff voice, his sage words imparting advice he'd picked up over the years, his calm manner, no matter what the situation. Most of all, she missed his worn, craggy face, the leathery skin brown as a walnut after years spent outside, his familiar musky smell, his scratchy whiskers that tickled her skin when he held her tight as she cried her heart out.

She'd found it hard to take over the tasks Bernardo had carried out. Tending the chickens, chopping wood, checking the fence around the coop in case foxes had tried to get in, keeping an eye on anything that needed repairing, as well as doing all her usual chores, was wearing her out. Rosa often got up before dawn and did some of them for her, but even though she was healthy for her age, she sometimes complained about her aching joints.

'You've lost weight,' Anna-Maria said, peering at her.

Sara had been half asleep, her spoon resting on the edge of the barely touched bowl of soup. She jerked awake at the sound of Anna-Maria's voice.

'You always were a skinny thing, but your clothes are hanging off you now.' She clicked her tongue, and frowned. 'And you're exhausted. It's not good for you. Tell her, Rosa.'

'I'm tired, that's all,' Sara protested.

'Too tired to eat,' Rosa commented.

'I'm not hungry.' Sara pushed the bowl away.

'You're working too hard,' Anna-Maria said. 'You have black shadows around your eyes, your hands are calloused, and you have bruises all over your legs and arms. You look terrible.'

Tears brimmed in Sara's eyes. She dashed them away, hurt. 'Thank you for the compliments.'

'Aw, I didn't mean to upset you. I was thinking that maybe you need a man, to help share some of the burden.'

'A man?'

'A husband. A soulmate.'

Sara snorted. 'I don't need a husband, or a soulmate, to share any burden. I'm happy as I am, and I can cope.' She held up her hand as Anna-Maria opened her mouth to speak again. 'That's the end of the subject. Now leave me to eat the rest of my soup in peace.'

But when she went to bed later that night, Anna-Maria's words rolled around her head, and her heart ached for someone to hold her close.

Sara came back from her trip to the village, her face flushed as she rushed indoors. 'I've decided to hire a woman from the village to help around the place,' she announced.

Rosa looked up from the sock she was darning. 'What? Why's that then?'

'I've realised I've too much to do here, what with preparing our remedies, seeing patients, and cleaning up in between each one. I thought that perhaps Anna-Maria is right, we need someone to help out with the things Nonno used to do.' Her voice wobbled slightly, but she carried on. 'Even in the winter, there are still so many chores.'

Anna-Maria coughed, then thumped her chest. 'How will you pay her?'

'With free meals and a bed to sleep in at night,' Sara replied.

'Good luck with finding someone,' Anna-Maria said, chuckling.

'I already have.'

'And who would that be?' Rosa put down her darning and glared at her. 'I really think you should have spoken to us first, if she's coming to live here.'

'I thought you wouldn't mind. It's Cassandra Barbieri.'

'Ah.'

The young woman was well known in the village. Her father had died when she was young, leaving her mother to bring up six children by herself. Friends and neighbours had helped out, but the children had grown up wild. They spent their days running about the mountains instead of going to school, despite their mother's attempts to beat them into submission. One by one, they'd left home over the years, until only Cassandra remained. Thin and wiry, her long black hair a mass of tangled curls, she nonetheless had the strength of a man.

Sara had learned that the mother had died the winter before and that, unused to being a part of society, Cassandra was struggling to survive. Sara thought that their cottage, tucked away in the forest, far from people, could be a place where the young woman would have a chance to heal and flourish. So she had taken a basket of sweet-smelling home-made food and gone to the tumbling-down wooden shack where Cassandra lived.

The girl had opened the door and eyed her suspiciously. 'What yer wan'?'

Sara took in Cassandra's unkempt appearance, the broken, grimy fingernails plucking nervously at a cotton dress that was more patches than the original material, and the smell of stale sweat and filth that emanated from the girl. She raised the basket. 'I've brought you something to eat.'

'Don't wannit.' Cassandra began to close the door.

'No, wait, don't go,' Sara said. 'You look starving, are you sure you don't want some bread and cheese? I think there are some dried grapes in there too. And some of Rosa's *cantucci*, you'll love them.' She smiled.

'*Cantucci*?' Cassandra took a step towards the basket and sniffed. Her eyes gleamed.

'All for you.' Sara held her breath, desperately hoping the girl would let her in the house.

'A'right.' She turned and went inside, leaving Sara on the doorstep.

Sara took it as a signal to follow, and went into the shack. There was a single room, like Anna-Maria's cottage, but the similarities ended there. Sara gazed around in horror at the mess. Broken furniture lay everywhere, together with dried remains of food and what appeared to be carcasses of animals. There was a grubby blanket and mattress in one corner of the room that had been kept clear, where Sara supposed the girl slept, and a small table and chair underneath a window, where she probably ate.

'Where shall I put it?' Sara asked, indicating the basket.

'Gi' it 'ere.' Cassandra darted over and snatched it from Sara's grasp, then put it on the floor next to the chair. The chair creaked as she sat down, its legs wobbling dangerously.

'Is it really for me?' Her eyes opened wide as she took out the food and placed it on the table before her.

'Of course.' Sara's heart broke as she watched Cassandra devour the food at an astonishing rate, barely stopping to take breath. 'When you've finished, I've got a proposal for you.'

'A wha'?' Cassandra asked, her mouth full of freshly made bread.

'Eat, and then we'll talk.' Sara stood and waited patiently until every morsel was gone. Cassandra licked her fingertips and picked up the crumbs that had spilled on the table, not wasting anything.

When she'd finished, Sara had quietly explained her idea to Cassandra. While the girl wasn't overly enthusiastic about leaving her home, the lure of home-made cake every day was too tempting, and she'd eventually agreed.

Now all Sara had to do was convince Rosa.

'Let's give her a chance,' she pleaded. 'She has nothing. We can teach her a trade, give her hope for her future.'

'We can't take in every waif and stray you come across,' Rosa grumbled.

'Rosa, please.'

'Oh, all right. Just this once, mind. It's your cottage, but we can't have it overrun with everyone you feel sorry for.'

'Thank you, Rosa.' Sara threw her arms around her and kissed her on the cheek. 'I'll go and get her, she's waiting outside.'

25

'I have to admit, you were right,' Rosa said begrudgingly. She was helping Sara tidy up the kitchen after another busy day of tending to patients. Pans clattered in the ceramic sink as she scrubbed them vigorously.

'About what?' Sara finished wrapping up the bandages and put them back in the box, ready for the morning.

'Young Cassandra.'

Sara turned to Rosa. 'You're actually saying I was right? Wonders will never cease.' Rosa had found it difficult to accept Cassandra at first, telling Sara that the girl would only bring them trouble.

'A woman can change her mind, can't she? Look at her out there.' She jerked her head at the window, where they could see Cassandra chopping wood. Chips flew around her as she worked in a ceaseless rhythm: picking up a log, placing it on the block, swinging the axe, throwing the splintered wood onto the pile, then on to the next one. Her wiry arms glistened with sweat, despite the cold evening air, and her long black hair flew around her head, giving her an ethereal appearance.

'She certainly works hard.' Sara hadn't regretted a single day since the girl had come to live at the cottage.

'And she scrubs up well, now that she's started washing herself and her clothes,' Rosa replied. 'She's made your life easier, I'll give her that. You're looking better, and you've put on some weight too.'

'I wish she'd trust us more,' Sara said with a sigh. Cassandra spoke little, her eyes never meeting theirs when they addressed her, and at mealtimes she would bolt down her food in silence and flee the cottage as soon as she finished. Sara had given her Bernardo's room, thinking the spartan style would appeal to the girl. Cassandra had taken one look at the bed and dragged the covers onto the floor. She had slept there ever since.

'She's wild, that one, you'll never change her,' Anna-Maria said. She often came to the cottage, to help Sara or make concoctions for the villagers, but never stayed overnight. 'The spirits need me,' she said whenever Sara tried to insist. 'I've never abandoned them before, and I'm not going to start now.' Sara hated the thought of the old woman walking to the cottage and back, but knew it was pointless arguing with her.

Anna-Maria looked over at Cassandra, still chopping wood. 'If you have no children of your own, you could do worse than teach the girl.'

'Let her become a healer?' Sara exclaimed.

'Either that, or you accept one of your suitors.'

Sara tutted. Several men from the village had proposed over the last year, but she'd turned every single one down.

'She's right,' Rosa said. 'If the Innocenti are to continue, you must marry someone.'

'There's still plenty of time,' Sara retorted, but she knew they were right.

'Don't take too long,' Anna-Maria said, chuckling.

Sara ignored the old woman's comment and tasted the stew

bubbling on the stove. 'It's about ready, I'll go and tell Cassandra to wash. And no more talk of suitors, you two, you're making me lose my appetite!'

To Sara's relief, Rosa and Anna-Maria were talking about cough remedies when she came back, Cassandra close on her heels. The girl's cheeks and hands were bright red from washing in the freezing cold water outside. Sara had tried to insist she washed in the kitchen, but Cassandra told her she preferred the outdoors to the stuffy cottage.

As usual, the girl bolted the stew down, barely stopping to chew between forkfuls and tearing chunks of bread off the loaf to mop up the gravy. After numerous attempts to teach Cassandra to eat more slowly, Sara had given up and accepted there were some things she would never be able to change about her. Rosa frowned at the noises coming from the girl, but said nothing as she primly ate her dinner. Sara hid a smile; Anna-Maria made similar sounds, her nearly toothless gums making hard work of chewing the pieces of meat, but Rosa would never have dreamed of saying anything.

They were still halfway through their meal when Cassandra leaped to her feet.

'I finished,' she mumbled. She took her plate to the sink and rinsed it, then ran out of the back door.

'Rude child.' Rosa snorted her disapproval. 'Mind you, with her upbringing, it's only to be expected.'

'I wonder where she goes every evening,' Sara said.

'Why don't you follow her and find out?' Rosa suggested.

'No, I can't do that,' Sara said. 'I remember when Mamma had the servants follow me everywhere, it was humiliating.'

'Because she thought you were up to no good,' Rosa replied.

Sara blushed. She still remembered her parents accusing her of meeting a boy in the woods, and how hurt she'd been by their cruel words.

'Ask her then.' Rosa put down the bone she'd been sucking, and licked her greasy fingers.

Sara collected the plates and took them over to the sink. 'All right, I will.'

✿

She got her chance the next morning. As she left the chicken coop, she saw Cassandra sitting on a log, steam rising from a cup she held in her hands. The sight of Cassandra's bare arms made Sara shiver, and she pulled her woollen cape around her more tightly.

'Aren't you cold?' she asked.

'Nah. 'Tis best time o' day.' Cassandra gave her a rare smile, showing gaps among her teeth. Sara had shown her how to care for them, but several were already missing.

'What are you drinking?' Sara gestured at the cup.

Cassandra looked down at the ground, her face flushed, her lips pressed tightly together.

'I'm sorry, I didn't mean anything by it.' Sara was mortified. 'I've told you already, you can help yourself to anything in the cottage. It's got a lovely aroma, that's all, and I was wondering what was in it.'

Cassandra jerked her head up. 'I took somethin' from t'pantry.'

'Is it good?'

'Taste?' She held the cup out to Sara.

She took a sip. 'Delicious. I can taste wormwood, rosemary and valerian, and I'm sure there's a hint of wild asparagus. Am I right?'

Cassandra nodded. 'There's one more.'

Sara sniffed deeply. 'Of course. Silver leaf. Very little, but I can smell it more than taste it. Do you make it every morning?'

'Uh huh. It helps.'

'Helps what?' She was interested to see if the girl had any healing powers.

'Speak to the dead.'

Sara felt a chill run through her. 'The dead?'

'At t'grave.'

'What grave?'

'Boy's grave, down by the river.'

'Will you show me?' Sara asked gently.

Cassandra stood and took the cup back from Sara. 'Come.'

They walked in silence through the woods, the early morning mist dissipating as the sun rose over the mountains. The trees gradually came to life with birdsong, and small animals darted about in the undergrowth. Sara recognised the path after a while, and wasn't surprised when they ended up in a familiar clearing.

'There.' Cassandra pointed at the gravestone Sara had come across some years before, fleeing from her grandfather's past. The two women walked over and stood, heads bowed, before the grave.

'Bob,' Sara said.

'You know 'im?'

'We met, once before.' Sara ran her hand over the marble, her fingertips brushing the inscription. *Bob. Faithful friend, in life and death.* 'He made me see sense.'

'He tells me things.'

Sara waited, but Cassandra didn't say anything else. 'How did you find this place?'

Cassandra shuffled her feet. 'One evenin'. I was sad.' She sighed. 'I miss my mamma.'

Sara wanted to put an arm around her, but refrained, unsure whether it would be welcome. 'I'm sorry,' she said instead.

'She died.'

'I heard.'

'Same day Lapo went.'

'Lapo?'

'My brother. 'Twas only me an' 'im, then Mamma died an' 'e wen' t'the quarry.'

'He left you all alone?'

''Ad to.' Cassandra picked a blade of grass and twisted it around her finger before adding, 'There was no work, see.'

'I understand.'

'But 'e 'elped me bury 'er, afore he left.'

'That's good.' Sara was relieved that at least the girl's brother had stayed long enough to help her with the burial.

Cassandra sniffed and wiped her nose with the back of her hand. 'Anyway, I was out walkin' one evenin' an' I 'eard a voice, callin' me.' She glanced at Sara, a defiant look on her face. Sara smiled and nodded encouragingly. 'It brought me 'ere. I like this place. It calms me. I come every night now.'

She'd never said so much all in one go before. 'What does Bob tell you?' Sara asked.

'Things.' She avoided Sara's eyes. ''Bout what's passed and what's t'come.'

'And drinking the tea helps?'

''E told me what to put in it. Said I would 'ear 'im better. An' I can.'

'Will you tell me what he says?'

Cassandra shook her head. 'I can't,' she whispered. 'Only I can know.'

Sara turned away, disappointed.

Cassandra put a hand on her arm. 'But I can tell you this. It's not your fault, you musn' blame yerself.'

'What's not my fault? Do you mean my parents?'

'That were never your fault.' Cassandra smiled sadly. 'An' neither is what's t'come.'

'Please, tell me so I can understand. What isn't my fault?' Sara begged. But Cassandra shook her head and spoke no more.

They remained at the graveside a while longer, both lost in their thoughts, then slowly made their way back to the cottage. It wasn't until Sara was almost asleep in bed later that she realised Cassandra hadn't answered her question.

26

The dragonfly flew over Sara's head and came to rest on the edge of the fountain, its wings vibrating gently. Sara got up from the ground, where she'd been clearing some weeds around a plant, and grimaced at the twinge in her back.

'You've returned then.' She brushed some hair out of her eyes and smiled at the insect. Somehow, she knew it was the same dragonfly she'd followed through the snow all those years before, when she'd discovered the cottage, although she wasn't sure how that could be possible.

It set about rubbing its front legs against its head and antennae, and she watched, fascinated. No matter how often she saw the dragonflies in the Grove, she remained captivated every time.

'Sara!' Rosa's voice interrupted her thoughts, startling both her and the dragonfly. It darted off and was soon out of sight among the fruit trees.

Sara sighed. 'Coming,' she called.

Rosa stood by the door, her face flustered. 'We have a guest,' she whispered in an urgent tone as Sara approached.

'A guest?'

'Keep your voice down.' She glanced at the cottage. 'I left him in the kitchen with Anna-Maria.'

'And who would our guest be?' Sara whispered back.

'It's Cassandra's brother, come to see his sister.'

'Her brother? After all this time?' Sara put her hands on her hips. 'I should give him a piece of my mind, abandoning poor Cassandra like that–'

'That's what he's come for,' Rosa interrupted. 'Says he had no choice, but now he wants to make amends.'

Sara snorted. 'Amends, eh? We'll see about that.' She strode forward, wrenched down the handle, and flung the door open.

'It's about time you turned up,' she said, hurrying across the room to the kitchen.

The man stopped talking to Anna-Maria and turned towards her. Kind hazel eyes peered out from under bushy black eyebrows, his face barely visible beneath his overgrown beard and matted dark-brown hair. He stood and stretched out his hand in greeting, and Sara noticed how his check cotton shirt and black trousers hung off his thin frame. His hands were grimy and calloused, but his grip was strong as he shook her hand.

'Apologies for my appearance, m'lady,' he said, dipping his head. 'I bin workin' in the quarry the last year or so, 'tis not a place for gettin' dressed up. I came as soon as I'd put by enough money for the two of us, 'bout four week ago now, 'twas. I left the quarry and come 'ome. I were worried for Cassie, all alone up at the cottage. I went there, but the neighbours told me she was 'ere.'

He spoke so humbly that Sara's anger dissipated. 'After your mother died last year, they helped Cassandra as much as possible, but she couldn't cope by herself.'

'Couldn't? She isn't–'

'No, please don't think that.' Sara gestured for him to sit back down, and pulled up a chair in front of him. 'I asked her to come and live with us a couple of months ago, and in return she helps with jobs around the house.'

'That's very kind of you, m'lady.' He picked at some dirt under a nail.

'Please, call me Sara. No one addresses me as m'lady or lady anymore. And you're Lapo, aren't you? Cassandra's told me about you.'

He frowned. 'I hope all good things, m– I mean, Sara.' He looked down at the table. 'Is Cassie aroun'? I'm goin' to stay, fix the cottage, work the land, now I've got some money. It's not much, but it should see us by for a while until we get settled.'

'She's gone to the village on some errands for me, but you're welcome to wait here for her.' Sara hesitated. 'I might have some clean clothes upstairs, and you can have a wash out by the pump, if you'd like.'

'Thank you, it'd be much 'preciated.'

'Wait here a moment.' Sara ran upstairs and got a towel from her wardrobe, then opened the large wooden chest where she kept Bernardo's things. His familiar scent wafted out of the chest and she sat down on the edge of her bed, overcome for a moment. She hadn't opened it since putting his things in there the day of his funeral, and her grief hit her, almost as potent as it had been three years before. She brushed away a tear and gathered herself, before going through his clothes. In the end she took out a grey cotton shirt Rosa had made for his last birthday, together with a pair of beige trousers he'd kept for 'best'. He hadn't worn either much, so Sara felt she wouldn't mind seeing the stranger downstairs wearing them.

'Here you go.' She handed him the bundle. 'The pump's over there, behind the coop. It's a sunny spot, so the water shouldn't be too cold, I hope. I've got some stew to warm up, would you like some?'

He seemed bemused, but nodded. 'Thanks. That would be great. I haven' eaten for a couple of days, I was in such a rush to get 'ere.'

Anna-Maria opened a cupboard and took out a pair of scissors. 'Here, give yourself a trim while you're at it,' she said, handing them to him.

He ran his fingers self-consciously through his hair, wincing as they got caught up in the tangles. 'Maybe I should.'

'Right, off you go then.' Sara opened the back door. 'By the time you're done, lunch will be ready.'

Sara was ladling stew onto the plates when the door opened again. She turned to ask if everything was all right, but stood and stared at him, speechless. Gone was the wild man of the mountains. The man standing inside the door had neatly combed hair that had been cut just below his ears, and his face was clean-shaven. Bernardo's clothes fitted him almost perfectly, and he no longer looked like a scarecrow.

Rosa bustled in behind him. 'There you go, told you it would be ready. Sit down, make yourself at home.'

Sara raised an eyebrow.

Rosa sidled over to her. 'I was out in the garden when I saw him getting cleaned up, and offered to help him. He looks a lot better, don't you think?' she said, her voice low.

Sara flushed. 'Oh, get on with you.' She turned to Lapo, trying to hide her confused feelings. 'Your sister should be here soon, then we can eat.'

There came the sound of someone scraping their boots outside, then Cassandra waltzed in, swinging her basket while humming a ditty.

'Speak of the devil,' Rosa exclaimed.

Lapo leapt to his feet. 'Cassie?'

She took one look at him and screamed. The basket fell to the floor as she stared at him, mouth wide open.

'Cassie?' His voice was quieter. He took a step forward, then stopped, a hand held out towards her.

Cassandra's face was flushed, her eyes glistening with tears. She shrank back, her fists clenched, then turned and fled outside. Lapo's shoulders slumped.

'Go on, boy, go after her,' Rosa ordered.

'She doesn't want me to,' he replied, his face glum.

'Don't be stupid. She's in shock, that's all. Go, tell her what you told us.'

He hesitated, then followed his sister outside.

Sara let out a huge sigh. 'Something tells me lunch will be late. I'll put the stew back on the stove.'

When they returned, Cassandra's eyes were red-rimmed and swollen. She gave Sara and Rosa a watery smile.

'Lapo says he'll stay 'ere now, no more quarry.'

'I know. It's wonderful, isn't it?'

'Yes.'

There was an awkward silence, until Rosa clapped her hands. 'Shall we eat this delicious stew then? Be a shame to waste it.'

Chairs scraped on the tiled floor as they sat down. Unable to resist any longer, there was silence as they ate. Sara glanced at Cassandra every now and then, puzzled by her reticence to talk to her brother. She made up her mind to speak with her as soon as she could.

27

Cassandra joined Sara in the Grove later that evening, and sat beside her on the edge of the fountain. They watched the sun set behind the mountains, the clouds glowing a fiery red as it disappeared from view.

'Is everything all right?' Sara asked. 'I don't wish to pry, but you don't seem very happy now Lapo's back.'

Cassandra sighed. It was hard to see her in the gloom, but Sara could hear her shuffling her feet. 'I'm pleased he's back.' She didn't sound too convinced.

'But?'

'T'other day, near the grave...'

'Bob's grave?'

'Yes. 'E told me somethin'.'

'And you can't tell me what he said.'

'No.'

'But it's not good.'

'No.'

'Can I do anything to help?'

'No.' This time her voice was a mere whisper.

'I'm sorry.' Sara patted the girl's hand. 'Perhaps you can talk to Lapo.'

'Perhaps.'

Something in her voice made Sara glance at her. Cassandra's expression was so filled with hate it took Sara's breath away. 'Cassie–'

'Don' call me that,' she snapped.

'Sorry.' Sara could feel the girl's rigid body next to hers. 'Cassandra, are you sure–?'

'Can we go inside now? I'm cold,' she interrupted.

Sara desperately wanted to help the girl, but didn't know what to do. 'Of course,' she replied, hating herself for not delving deeper. She took off her shawl and wrapped it around Cassandra's shoulders.

'Thanks,' she mumbled through chattering teeth.

'It's the least I can do.' Sara paused. 'I'm here whenever you'd like to talk,' she added softly. Cassandra didn't reply.

As they left the Grove Sara looked for the dragonflies, but they were nowhere to be seen. She wondered briefly where they could be, then gathered her skirts and hurried after Cassandra.

Sara imagined Cassandra had only needed time to get used to having her brother back; she saw that the girl rushed off after finishing her chores whenever she could. Caught up in the comings and goings of her patients, when she noticed that Cassandra was quieter than ever she put it down to the young girl feeling overwhelmed with relief.

'That's some bruise you have, girl,' Rosa remarked one day.

Sara looked up from Signor Rossi's bunion, and frowned. Reaching up to a cupboard, Cassandra's top had risen, and a dark purple bruise was clearly visible on the right of her lower back.

'What happened?' she asked.

Cassandra hastily pulled down her top, a sullen look on her face. 'Was helpin' Lapo,' she said, her cheeks flushing. 'Bumped into a board he was movin'.'

'Rosa, give her that pot of arnica over there.' Sara gestured to the dresser, where they often left the more commonly used remedies. 'Put it on two or three times a day, it will help.'

Cassandra nodded, and took the pot without saying a word. Sara noticed a glint of anger in her eyes and wondered what was wrong.

'So I've got to drink this nettle tea a couple of times a day, and put on a poultice in the evening?' Signor Barbieri said, distracting her.

'What? Yes. You can put the poultice on morning and evening if it's painful. The rosemary and calendula are very soothing.' Sara concentrated on her patient and pushed any concerns about Cassandra to the back of her mind.

The rest of the day passed by in a flurry of coughs and colds, aching backs, broken fingers, a child with a pebble firmly wedged in each nostril, various cuts, bruises, and crushed nails, and a myriad of other complaints that kept her busy until the sun went down.

Lapo came to the cottage that evening, as he often did. Sara looked forward to his visits; once he'd got over his initial shyness, he was surprisingly good company. After a long day tending to patients, making more concoctions, and practising recipes, it was a relief to sit down and listen to his tales of life at the quarry.

She could close her eyes and be whisked away to a different world, one full of dust, dirt, hard labour and an even harder life, it was true, but it was also a world of camaraderie, friendships born around a log fire under starlit skies, little incidents that brought respite to the hardship.

'We was sittin' under a tree, eatin' our soup with bread so 'ard you'd break yer teeth if you tried to eat it wi'out soaking it first,' he said. The weather was warmer, and they often stayed outside in the garden until late, shawls over their shoulders to keep the chilly night air at bay, listening to Lapo talk while he drank a glass of whisky. His voice became richer and softer, and he leaned back in his chair, half closing his eyes.

'It were more water than soup, truth be told, wi' no meat and only little vegetables. But it were food, and we was starvin'. All you could 'ear was slurpin' and chompin', we was too 'ungry to talk. Then we 'eard a splosh, and ol' Ambrogio yellin'.' He chuckled. 'Turned out a beetle from the tree 'ad fallen in 'is soup and was swimmin' across the bowl. 'E was bashin' it with 'is spoon, tryin' to fish it out, but the bugger kep' gettin' away. So in the end 'e said, "Sod this", opened 'is mouth an' poured the soup in, beetle an' all.'

Rosa put her hand over her mouth. 'Ugh,' she squealed, squirming in her seat. 'He ate it?'

'We could 'ear 'im crunchin' it up afore 'e swallowed it,' Lapo said, laughing. 'But you know wha'? The funny thing is, we was all jealous of 'im. See, 'e got some meat, while all we got was some water with leaves floatin' in it. After tha', we all tried to sit under the tree, see if we got a beetle too.'

As she laughed with the others, Sara found herself staring at his clean-shaven face, the way his eyes crinkled at the corners whenever he smiled, and her gaze travelled down his neck to his collarbone. She flushed, a warm sensation flowing through her body. It took her a few moments to understand what it was. Love.

28

Spring arrived in a whirl of scented blossoms and new leaves, dewdrops glistening on spiderwebs in the early morning sun, and cool, crisp mornings that melted into warm days. The garden was alive with new growth, the plants flourished, and the wildlife came out of hibernation after the long, harsh winter.

Sara made her way down through the garden, pleased to see everything thriving. Anna-Maria walked beside her, her basket already full of green shoots she would add to their dinner later.

'You've worked hard these last few years and done wonders with the garden, child,' the old woman remarked as they watched a thrush hop across their path, a snail in its beak. It found a large stone and set about knocking the snail against it, finally breaking its shell and flying off triumphant with its prize.

'It's all thanks to Bernardo's hard work,' Sara replied. 'He did so much before he died.' Tears came to her eyes, as they always did whenever she spoke about her grandfather.

'He was a good man.'

Sara sniffed. 'Do you sense him sometimes, Anna-Maria?'

The old woman narrowed her eyes. 'Why do you ask?'

'Because I don't,' Sara replied sadly. 'When I first arrived here I could sense my grandmother's spirit. I saw her at times, too. But since Nonno died, I can't sense anything. Only a bleak emptiness.'

Anna-Maria took Sara's hand in her own calloused one, the skin paper thin and threaded with blue veins. 'That's because she's at peace, with herself and her past. She's with Bernardo now, where she belongs, and they've both moved on. She's no longer tied to the cottage. For that you should be thankful. Many spirits remain in torment for centuries before finding their peace. Some never do.'

'I understand.' Sara sighed. 'But I feel so alone.'

'Alone? You are surrounded by people who love you.'

'I know. But sometimes I wish...' She hesitated.

'For what?'

'For something more. For someone, who can fill the emptiness in my heart.'

Anna-Maria chuckled. 'I think perhaps your "someone" may be close by. I may be old, but my eyes still see perfectly well.'

'I'm sorry to tell you your eyes are failing you in this case. Here, come into the Grove and take whatever you need.' Sara stopped when the old woman didn't follow her through the gate. 'What's wrong?'

'The dragonflies,' Anna-Maria whispered. 'Where are they?'

The Grove was exceptionally still. No brightly coloured insects flitted among the plants or over their heads, none drank from the fountain at the centre. Even the birds were absent.

'I don't know.' Sara was lost for words. Never, in all the time she'd lived at the cottage, had the dragonflies been missing.

Anna-Maria stepped back, cowering. 'There's something bad here,' she whispered, her voice shaking. 'I've felt it before, but never like this, never this strong.'

'That's impossible.' Sara tried to laugh, but the frightened expression on the old woman's face stopped her. 'Come now, it's too early for the dragonflies. The Grove will soon be covered with them, wait and see.' But a cold fear travelled through her. *Her* dragonfly was missing too.

That afternoon, Sara set off to Cassandra's old wooden shack with Rosa's freshly baked *schiacciata* stuffed with slices of ham in her basket. She thought they would enjoy the soft bread, brushed with olive oil and sprinkled with salt; it had always been a favourite of hers when growing up at the villa. The sun was warm, not too hot, and it was a pleasant walk through the village.

The sound of a hammer on wood reached her as she strode along the path towards the shack. It was cooler under the shade of the trees, and the breeze blew her hair around her face.

'Hello,' she called out. 'It's Sara, I've brought you something to eat.'

The hammering stopped, and Lapo leaned over the side of the roof. 'Be right down!'

Sara peered inside the shack, but there was no sign of Cassandra. She stepped through the door, blinking as her eyes grew accustomed to the gloomy interior. She saw the mattress in the corner had a clean blanket pulled over it, and the room appeared tidier.

'Somethin' smells delicious.'

Sara jumped. She turned to see Lapo leaning against the frame, his tanned upper body naked, a smile on his face. She felt her cheeks growing hot, and hoped he wouldn't notice.

'Rosa made some *schiacciata* after lunch. I thought you might like some, so I added sliced ham and olives. I hope that's all right.'

'O' course.' He picked a shirt up off a nearby chair and threw it on, then rubbed his hands together in anticipation. 'Shall we go outside?'

Sara followed him over to an ancient olive tree, its gnarled branches creating a canopy above their heads, trying to get the image of his body out of her mind.

'Isn't Cassandra here?' Sara put the basket on the ground and lifted out the contents, putting them on a nearby rock. She handed Lapo a piece of *schiacciata* wrapped in a clean cloth.

He didn't answer but took an enormous bite, eyes closed, and chewed. 'Heaven,' he said after a couple of minutes. He opened his eyes. 'Cassie's not 'ere, no. Did she say she was comin'?'

'Oh, no. She runs off the minute she finishes her chores, I assumed she came here to help you with repairs.'

Lapo frowned. 'Not today. She's a bit wild, that 'un, needs some tamin'.' He ate another mouthful of *schiacciata*.

'She's been alone a while, she needs to get used to having someone around again,' Sara pointed out.

He narrowed his eyes, a muscle working in his jaw. He opened his mouth to speak, then shook his head. His expression softened. 'Well, she's missin' out on somethin' good 'ere.' He licked his fingers, greasy with olive oil. 'Not got any more, do you?'

'There's plenty in the basket, help yourself.'

She studied him as he ate, noting the dark stubble on his face, his hair sprinkled with flecks of sawdust, his calloused hands grimy after a hard day's work. His patched trousers were held up by a belt with a metal buckle, and his worn shoes had the slightly pungent smell of the castor oil he rubbed into the cracked leather to keep it supple.

'Penny for 'em?'

'Oh.' Flustered, Sara desperately tried to think of something to say. 'I see you were hungry.'

'Hard work builds up an appetite,' he said. 'You not eatin' any?'

'I ate some earlier.'

'Go on. 'Ere.' He thrust the *schiacciata* at her.

Giggling, Sara took a bite, savouring the salty, oily taste. 'It tastes better when you eat it outdoors.' She smiled at him.

'You got oil on your chin.' He leaned over and rubbed it off with his thumb.

Sara froze. His face was mere inches away. She could smell the olives and ham on his breath, see the miniscule beads of sweat on his skin, the way his pupils dilated as he stared at her. He cupped her cheek with his calloused hands, the rough skin making hers tingle. Then he shifted, and suddenly his lips were on hers, firm against her softness, insistent and commanding. She closed her eyes, basking in the warm sensation that filled her body, floating up into the branches of the olive tree, as his hands caressed her neck and her breasts.

Something flitted close to their heads, wings beating frantically. Lapo batted it away, but it came back, more insistent. Sara saw it was a dragonfly, and struggled to sit up.

Lapo leaned over her, gazing at her with dark eyes full of emotion. 'Shall we go inside?'

She glanced at the dragonfly.

'Ignore it, damn thing.'

She hesitated, then nodded. He held out his hand and helped her to her feet. Sara heard the faint vibration of wings near her ear but paid no more heed to the dragonfly, her mind elsewhere.

She lay beneath the blanket, a thin layer of sweat covering her body, her limbs languid and heavy. She reached over and put her hand on Lapo's chest, unsure what to do. Her mother's voice spoke inside her head, loud and insistent. *You little whore. What next? Are you going to tell us you're carrying a bastard child, perhaps?* Sara pulled away, tugging the blanket around her more tightly, suddenly ashamed. He lay on his back, his face half hidden in the shadows of the room.

Her mind still whirling with her mother's condemnation, she blurted out, 'Was it... Was I...?'

He didn't move, didn't reach out for her, didn't take her in his arms. ''Twas all right,' he grunted.

Sara snatched her hand from his chest, shame flooding her, and tears pricked at her eyes. She burrowed further under the blanket, humiliated that she hadn't been enough for him, and knew she'd never be enough. Her parents had made sure of that all those years before.

'What's wrong?' he asked, frowning.

'I-I tried my best,' she sobbed, tears rolling down her cheeks. All the pent-up emotions she'd been holding back since the day they'd met burst free, mingled with embarrassment and guilt. She leapt to her feet, clutching the blanket, and looked wildly around for her clothes.

'I didn' mean noth–' Lapo said, but stopped as Sara grabbed one of his shoes and threw it at him.

'M-my mother w-warned me against men like you,' she said, hiccoughing. 'Only wanting one thing, casting you aside when they're done.' She found her dress and pulled it over her head, letting go of the blanket.

'Don' throw things at me.' He glared at her, then scrabbled around for his clothes, tugging on his trousers and shirt.

She finished dressing. 'I'm going now, while I still have some dignity left.'

'Go then, you slut.' He spat the last word with venom.

She reeled back from the sneer of disgust on his face. 'What did you call me?'

'Slut. You're the same as all t'other whores, no matter how fancy you pretends t'be.'

Sara stared at him, stunned. The red-faced man before her bore no resemblance to the man who had tenderly made love to her only a short while before.

'Go, I said!' He took a step towards her, his fist raised.

Terrified, Sara turned and fled. As she reached the door, it slammed open. Sara stared at the girl in the doorway.

'Cassie. What are you doin' 'ere?' Lapo snapped.

''Tis my house,' she retorted. 'What's wrong? I heard shoutin' from outside.'

'Nothin',' he growled back. 'Go away. Sara was jus' leavin'.'

Cassandra looked from her brother to Sara, and back again. 'Somethin' happen?'

'I said go away!' Lapo shouted.

Cassandra flinched. 'Sara?'

Sara avoided the girl's eyes. 'Nothing happened. It was just a misunderstanding. I've got to get going now. I'll see you back at the cottage, Cassandra.' She brushed past the girl, ignoring Lapo, and ran outside. She didn't stop running until she was almost home.

29

The embers in the fire glowed softly, emitting only a slight warmth. Sara sat in her armchair, her shawl wrapped around her shoulders. A distant church bell struck two. The cottage was silent; Rosa had gone to bed at ten, tired of waiting up for Cassandra to return. Sara had been too agitated to sleep, confused thoughts whirling around her mind. She'd made a herbal tea, but it hadn't helped much.

She could still hear her mother's voice, after all these years. That day they'd accused her of slipping off to the woods to meet a boy, as if she were some kind of scarlet woman. Her face burned at the memory, whether in anger or humiliation, she wasn't sure. For many long years she'd never even so much as looked at a man in that way. Not until Lapo had arrived, with his dark good looks, those eyes that seemed to gaze into her soul, and his open, friendly manner that was so different from his wilder sister.

Sara had given her body and her heart to him, and he had mocked her in return.

Her mother had been right all along. Never again would she let a man close to her. *But what about the healers?* a voice whispered in her head. *Who will carry on the work when you are gone?* She clenched her fists, confusion reigning as she attempted to make sense of what had happened that afternoon. She suddenly remembered the dragonfly that had appeared before she'd gone into the shack. Had it been trying to warn her? She pushed the heels of her hands against her eyes, trying to get rid of the images burned in her mind.

When the back door creaked open, Sara jumped. She looked up and saw a shadow slip inside, quietly closing the door behind it.

'Who's there?' she called out.

There was a small shriek.

'Cassandra?'

'Sara, you startled me!' Cassandra approached, clasping her hand to her chest.

'Come and sit by the fire. The days are warm, but the nights are still chilly.' Sara grabbed the poker and stirred up the dying embers. Flames sparked back into life, creating a little heat in the cold room. 'Sit here, I'll get you a blanket.' Cassandra was still wearing the cotton dress from earlier; it was perfect for the warm spring days, but not heavy enough for the colder nights.

Sara tutted as she wrapped the blanket around her. 'You'll catch your death–' She stopped as Cassandra gave a small cry of pain, and noticed the girl's forehead was beaded with sweat. 'What's wrong?'

'N-nothing.' She shifted slightly, and winced.

Sara crouched before her, holding a candle. 'You're hurt. Let me see.'

Cassandra shook her head. She clutched her dress more tightly about her. 'It's only a bruise.'

'Do you want to tell me what happened?'

Cassandra remained silent, her knuckles white from gripping the material.

Sara pursed her lips. 'Does it hurt when you breathe in?'

'A little.' She gave a small gasp as Sara ran a hand over her ribs.

'It would seem more than a little. It feels swollen too, although I can't be sure if you won't let me look at it.' Cassandra pulled back. 'I won't insist,' Sara said. 'But your rib may be broken. If it still hurts in the morning, you'll have to let me look at it properly. In any case, I want you to rest for a few days and we'll see how it goes.'

'Rest? But what about my chores?' Cassandra struggled to sit up, then fell back with a whimper, clutching her side.

'You won't be doing any chores for a while,' Sara said firmly.

'Don't send me away,' Cassandra whispered.

'No, of course not. You can't go home now, not while your brother is still repairing your cottage.'

She lay her head against the back of the armchair. 'Thank you.'

Sara touched the girl's forehead. 'You haven't got a fever, which is good. But it's probably best you sleep down here tonight, I'll prepare a bed for you. I'll make you a tea as well, it will take some of the pain away and help you sleep.'

It didn't take her long to put clean sheets on the spare mattress they kept for patients, and move it in front of the fire, where it was warm. While Sara waited for the saucepan of water to boil, she pondered over Cassandra's injury. The girl hadn't wanted to tell her about it, and Sara couldn't understand why. Had she planned to carry on as if nothing had happened? She put some willow bark into a cup and poured the water over it. While it was steeping, she went to the pantry for a pot of arnica ointment. Once the tea was ready, she carried everything over to Cassandra.

'Here, drink this.'

Cassandra took the cup and made a face.

'I've put some honey in it, it won't taste horrible, I promise,' Sara said.

The girl drank some and smiled. 'It tastes sweet.'

'I told you so. Drink it all up.' Sara waited until Cassandra had finished. 'Right, give me the cup and I'll help you onto the mattress.'

It wasn't easy to move Cassandra without hurting her, but eventually she lay in front of the fire, grimacing in pain.

'This is arnica, it will help the bruising. Put it on a couple of times a day.' She handed Cassandra the pot, then sat in the armchair next to her. 'So, are you going to tell me how it happened?'

''Twas an accident.'

'I should hope so.'

'I wasn't payin' attention.'

'To what?'

Cassandra clamped her mouth shut.

'Please, Cassandra, I need to know what happened.'

'I'm too tired.' Cassandra yawned and closed her eyes.

Sara sighed. 'We'll talk tomorrow then.' She tucked the blanket around Cassandra. 'Sleep tight.'

'Make sure bed bugs don' bite,' she mumbled, already half asleep.

Sara returned to the armchair and sat deep in thought.

Sara awoke to the sound of Rosa bustling around the kitchen, getting breakfast ready. She glanced over at Cassandra, who was still fast asleep. She got up with a quiet groan, her muscles stiff after sitting in the armchair all night, and joined Rosa in the kitchen.

'When did young 'un get in?' Rosa asked. She gestured to the table. 'Sit yourself down, I'll get you your tea.'

'I need to stretch my legs.' Sara busied herself cutting some bread and put it on the table, together with a pot of jam and a slab of butter. 'She got in late, I heard the clock strike two.'

'Two?' Rosa exclaimed.

'Shh.' Sara put her finger to her lips. 'She's injured, but she won't let me take a look. I gave her some willow bark tea, she's been sleeping ever since.'

Rosa lowered her voice. 'How on earth did she do it?'

'She wouldn't tell me.'

'What do you think happened?'

'I've no idea. It was dark, I couldn't see her properly by candlelight. But I think she's hiding something.'

'Maybe you should go and speak to Lapo.'

'Why him?' Her words came out harsher than she intended.

Rosa narrowed her eyes. 'Perhaps the girl will tell you everything when she's had a good sleep.'

'I hope so. I'm going to the Grove after breakfast.' Sara needed to get out of the cottage and spend some time alone, to put her thoughts in order.

'All right. But remember Signora Pellegrini will be here at half past nine, try to be back by then.'

'I completely forgot.' Sara ran her hand through her hair. 'There's the packet of herbs to prepare, and the cream is in the pantry, it just needs putting in a pot–'

'Calm down, Sara. I'll get everything ready.'

Sara smiled at her. 'Thank you. I don't know what I'd do without you. Be sure to prepare enough for a month; she needs to drink at least one infusion every morning, and put the cream on three times a day.'

'Don't you fuss, I'll see to everything. Now eat your breakfast and do whatever you have to do, otherwise there'll be a queue of patients all the way back to Gallicano!'

30

I t was a dull, grey day, the clouds so low they almost touched the treetops. In the distance the sun's rays burst through the clouds, lighting up the valley below. But up in the mountains, there was only the constant drip of condensation falling off leaves. The air was heavy and silent in the Grove; no birds sang and no insect stirred.

Sara was glad of her shawl. After the recent warm weather, the damp, chilly air seeped through to her bones. She placed her basket on the ground and looked around. The Grove was strangely bare without the dragonflies; it was as though all the magic had gone from the place. Then she felt it. A subtle undercurrent, like a soft vibration deep underground, rising up through the earth to the surface and breaking free with a malignant sigh. The hairs on her arms stood on end. She shivered, suddenly afraid. Of what, she wasn't sure.

'If only you were here,' she whispered, but she had no idea whether she meant the dragonflies, her grandfather, or her parents. *Perhaps all of them*, she thought.

She placed her basket on the ground and took out the blunt knife she used to dig up weeds. A couple of hours working in the

Grove would help take her mind off things. She hummed a tune as she cleared the weeds from under the bush in front of her, lost in her thoughts.

'Sara.'

She turned. Lapo stood a short distance away, turning his cap in his hands.

'I have nothing to say to you. I think you should leave.'

'I wanted to explain. You wouldn't let me finish yesterday, I–'

'You said more than enough.' Sara stood, barely aware she was still holding the knife.

'But...' He twisted the cap, a frantic expression on his face. 'I didn' mean those things, then Cassie arrived an–'

Sara didn't want to listen to his excuses. 'You made your feelings about me abundantly clear. Speaking of Cassandra, what happened to her after I left?'

'What d'you mean?'

'She came back to the cottage late last night, or rather in the early hours of the morning, and she was hurt. I wondered if you knew anything.'

'Hurt?' He shook his head, frowning. 'She seemed all right when she was with me.'

'She didn't hurt herself?'

Lapo narrowed his eyes. 'What 'as she said?'

'Nothing. She won't tell me anything. I think she's got a bruise on her side, and perhaps a broken rib, but I can't be sure as she won't let me look at it. I thought maybe you would know something?'

He shuffled his feet, his gaze shifting to the ground. 'It might've 'appened when we was up on the roof.'

'On the roof? What was she doing up there?'

'I was finishin' off, an' she come up the ladder, said she'd 'elp me pick up me tools. I told 'er to leave 'em, but you know what she's like. Said she was starvin', quicker we tidied up, quicker we'd eat somethin'.' He shrugged. 'She was pickin' up the hammer when she slipped.'

'What? She fell off the roof?'

'No, not really. I caught 'er just afore she went over, but she must've banged 'er side.'

'Oh. That would explain the bruise. And the rib.'

'How bad is she?'

'I've told her to rest for a few days, until we see how it goes. She was lucky she didn't fall.'

'Good.' He took a step forward.

Sara held up her hand. Something about him didn't feel right; he wouldn't look straight at her, and his shoulder twitched every now and then.

'Didn't your mother fall, the day she died?' A cold chill ran through Sara as she spoke. It was her voice, but she was no longer in control of the words she uttered.

'I don' know. I left in the mornin', Cassie said she died later that afternoon. Poor girl, havin' to cope with tha' all alone. I wish I could've bin there.'

Sara recalled her conversation with Cassandra one cold day in February in the Grove, and the girl telling her that Lapo had helped her bury their mother. And then she pictured the furious expression on his face the day before, the anger in his voice when he called her a slut, his arm raised to strike her, and she knew. 'Liar.'

'Wha'?' He looked confused. 'No, 'tis the truth.'

'What really happened, Lapo?' It was no longer her voice, but that of another woman, a woman who had lived many centuries earlier. Sara should have been scared, but all she felt was a detached curiosity, as if watching from a safe haven. 'Do you want to tell me your secret?'

He staggered backwards, as if she had struck him. 'Who are you, a witch?'

'No. But I can see inside you, right into your heart. I know, Lapo.' Images flashed before her, of Lapo, raging at his mother, and Cassandra huddled in a corner, imploring him to stop, then Lapo shoving their mother to the ground, hitting and kicking her, over and over until she no longer moved. 'You killed her.'

His face contorted into a snarl, and he lunged at her. His fist landed on the side of her head, and she fell to the ground, dazed. He leaned over her, his face only inches from hers, fury in his eyes.

'You know nothin'. She was askin' for it, just like Cassie was askin' to be hit. You *women*,' he spat the word, harsh and bitter, 'always interferin', never keepin' your mouths shut. You don't know when to stop.' His fingers dug into her arms as he moved his body on top of hers and pinned her to the ground. 'I liked you, Sara, but in the end, you're jus' like them. A woman should be seen an' never heard, if she knows what's good for her.'

He let go of her arms and put his hands around her throat. Her scream was abruptly cut off as he squeezed. Sara wriggled, struggling to get free, but his body was crushing her. Dots of light flashed before her eyes as she choked, desperate for air. Her hand scrabbled at his, scratching, drawing blood as she tried with all her strength to free herself. She managed to move a little to the side, but his fingers dug into her throat. She lifted her other hand and shoved him in the ribs, trying to push him off her.

He grunted and looked down at her, his eyes wide open. He relaxed his grip on her throat and she wriggled out from under him, then gasped with shock when she saw the handle of her knife protruding from his side.

'What have you done?' he whispered, his face white. He reached across and put his hand on the knife. Blood oozed out of the wound, coating his fingers.

'No!' Sara scrambled to her feet. 'Don't pull it out. Let me help you.'

'Witch.' He spat at her. 'Stay away.' He turned and fled from the Grove, a hand clasped to his side, leaving smears of blood on the hedge and gate.

'Lapo,' Sara shouted, but it was too late. He was gone.

Sara stumbled through the woods, following the smears of blood on leaves and bushes. She realised she was following the path to the river; she recognised a tree that had been struck by lightning, its charred branches lifeless among the green foliage. She slowed as she reached the clearing with the grave, a sense of foreboding coming over her. A twig snapped beneath her foot, startling her. She pushed a branch aside and stepped into the clearing.

Lapo lay, face down, across Bob's grave, still gripping the knife in his hand. Blood pooled beneath him, soaking his shirt and trousers, dripping off the edge of the tombstone. At first Sara thought he was dead, then she saw his back rise and fall. He was alive, if barely. Her healer instincts took over and she ran to him.

'Lapo.'

He made a gurgling noise and blood bubbled from his lips. Sara knelt beside him. There was nothing she could do, he was too close to death. For all his faults, she felt pity as she gazed down upon the dying man. She knew that violence was learned, passed down from generation to generation; young boys who saw their fathers beat their mothers often became wife-beaters themselves. It was a blight of their times, one she couldn't see ending during her days on this earth. She smoothed his hair and softly sang a lullaby Rosa had sung to her when she was little, hoping it would help the passing of his soul.

Her song finished, a quiet calm fell over the clearing. Nothing moved, no leaf fluttered in the breeze, no insect scuttled by in the undergrowth, and the birds were silent. Everything stopped, waiting for the end.

'I forgive you,' she whispered.

He gave a final sigh, and moved no more.

31

Sara's sense of dread increased as she approached the cottage. The thought of having to tell Cassandra and Rosa what had happened down at the Grove weighed heavily on her. She'd had to leave Lapo's body on Bob's grave, unable to move it. She would need assistance if he was to have a proper burial.

She stood at the door of the cottage, taking a moment to gather her thoughts, then reached out and turned the handle.

'There you are!' Rosa rushed over as soon as Sara stepped through the door.

'Is something wrong?' Sara asked, shocked at the other woman's appearance. Her hair, usually neatly pulled back into a bun, blew in wisps about her head, and she stood wringing her hands, an anguished look on her face.

'It's Cassandra. She's not breathing right. I came down to the Grove to find you, but you weren't there. I called and called. Where have you been? Is that blood on your hands?' Rosa stared at her, shocked.

Sara glanced down, grimacing at the sight of dried blood. 'I- it's nothing. I'll explain later. Let me see to Cassandra first.' She quickly washed her hands in the kitchen sink, before going over to the girl.

Cassandra lay on the mattress in front of the fire where Sara had left her only a few hours earlier, her face pale, her breathing coming in painful gasps. Beads of sweat coated her brow, and her hair was damp.

Sara touched the back of her hand to the girl's forehead. 'She's burning with fever.'

'I know. I've tried giving her some willow bark tea, but she vomited it back up,' Rosa said. 'She was coughing earlier, and now she's breathing funny like that.'

'It's her ribs.'

'Can you do something?'

'I don't know.' Sara stroked Cassandra's hair. 'Fetch me a bowl of cold water and a cloth, we'll see if we can bring her fever down.'

As Rosa bustled away, Cassandra opened her eyes. 'Mamma?'

'No, it's me, Sara.'

Cassandra smiled. 'I thought it was Mamma, come to get me,' she whispered. She tried to lift her head, but fell back, coughing.

'Lie down and stay still,' Sara said, worried. Rosa carried over a bowl of water with elder flowers, willow bark and silver leaf floating in it, and passed her a towel. 'Thank you.'

Cassandra seemed to settle as Sara bathed her face and neck with the damp towel. Her cough subsided, although her breathing was still laboured.

'It hurts,' she said, her hand fluttering over her chest.

'I know. You must stay still.' Sara took a clean cloth, placed the corner in the bowl, then dripped some of the healing tea onto Cassandra's dry, cracked lips.

'Tastes good.' She opened her mouth, and Sara let her have a few more drops.

'That's enough for now, we don't want to make you sick.' She took Cassandra's hand in hers. 'Try to sleep.'

She stood, fighting back the tears.

Rosa put an arm around her. 'Will she make it?'

'I don't know.' Sara clenched her fists. 'I feel so powerless at times like this. All we can do is wait. I've done what I can, it's up to her now. But her injuries are so bad...'

'Come, sit down and eat something.'

'I can't. I-I have to do something.'

'Nothing's so urgent you can't have a bite to eat,' Rosa insisted. She ushered Sara over to the kitchen table. 'Sit yourself down while I get you some food.'

A cup of tea was already waiting, and Sara sipped it gratefully while Rosa put some bread and jam on a plate. She sat and waited while Sara ate, her arms folded primly across her chest.

'Now, tell me all about it.'

Sara swallowed the last mouthful of bread and pushed the plate away. 'Let's go outside.' Without waiting for Rosa to follow her, she went to the door and out onto the steps. Rosa joined her shortly after.

'I couldn't tell you in there, in case Cassandra heard.' Sara ran her hands through her hair. 'There's no easy way to say this. Lapo's dead.'

'What?' Rosa glanced at the door, then back to Sara. She lowered her voice. 'You'd better tell me what happened.'

'I don't know where to start,' Sara said, her voice breaking.

'From the beginning,' Rosa said softly.

'All right.' Sara gathered her thoughts. The last hour or so was still a muddle in her mind. 'He attacked me, down at the Grove.'

'He attacked you?' Rosa stared at Sara, horrified.

Sara leaned back so Rosa could see the red marks around her neck.

'For the love of God, why?'

'I-I'm not sure.' The memories of their meeting in the Grove were vague, like wisps of fog blowing around her mind. She could still hear that other voice, revealing Lapo's secrets. 'He killed their mother.'

'How do you know that?'

'The healer, she told me.' She saw the confusion on Rosa's face. 'I can't explain, I'm sorry. But I know he killed their mother, and hurt Cassandra yesterday.'

'*He* did that to the poor girl?'

Sara nodded.

A flush of red covered Rosa's chest and neck. 'If he wasn't dead already, I'd...' She paused. 'How did he die? What happened?'

Sara leaned against the wall of the cottage, taking comfort from the cold stone. 'It was an accident. I was digging up weeds when he attacked me. He pushed me to the ground and put his hands around my neck. He was strangling me, I couldn't breathe, and–' Sara wiped her hand across her brow. She felt faint. 'I don't know how it happened, but I s-stabbed him.'

Rosa's mouth dropped open. 'You what?'

'Stabbed him. I was still holding the knife I was using for weeding.'

'You killed him? In the Grove?'

Sara shook her head. 'He ran off.'

'He was still alive?'

'Yes. I told him to let me help, but he ran away into the woods. I followed, but by the time I found him it was too late. He died soon after.'

'You know how this is going to look.' Rosa clasped her hands to her chest. 'They're going to say you killed him.'

'And I'm going to put things right.'

Rosa looked scared. 'How can we–?'

'Not us. Me. You have to stay with Cassandra.'

'But–'

Sara stood. 'She needs you.'

A voice came from behind them. 'Cassandra needs you both. Everything else comes later.' They turned to see Anna-Maria. 'What are you waiting for? Indoors, the pair of you.'

Cassandra was burning with fever. She mumbled something, then shifted in her sleep, wincing at the pain. Sara held her hand, to let her know she wasn't alone.

Anna-Maria crooned softly in the background, and Sara recognised the song she used to help souls find their way to the afterlife. She wept quietly, as Cassandra's breathing grew slower and shallower.

'I know what Lapo did, to you and your mother,' Sara whispered into the girl's ear. 'I'm so sorry I didn't understand what he was like. But you can rest in peace now, he won't hurt anyone ever again.' She felt a gentle pressure as Cassandra squeezed her hand.

'Thank you.' It was the merest whisper, translucent words fluttering away in the air like a dragonfly's wings, but Sara heard them and kept them locked within her heart.

Cassandra's eyes closed as she took her last breath, and Anna-Maria's song was the only sound in the room.

32

S ara stood at the door of the pantry, surveying the shelves before her. She knew exactly what she needed, but it was with a heavy heart that she selected the ingredients and took them back to the kitchen.

It was a Sunday morning, their one day off. Rosa had gone to Mass down at the village, and had said she would visit Anna-Maria as well, so Sara knew she had a few hours to herself. This was the perfect time to do it. The risks involved were great, as she knew, but she had no choice. She tried not to think about what could go wrong, about the fact that she could die. When she discovered she was carrying Lapo's child, her only thought had been to get rid of it.

She had argued with herself for days. She was alone, unmarried, with no daughter to continue as a healer after her, and she knew the chance may never come again. But she also remembered the lack of dragonflies whenever he was near, the way he had attacked her in the Grove, and what he had done to his own mother and sister. Sara couldn't bear his child. She despaired of ever being able to look at it, let alone love it.

Sara weighed out the herbs and put them into a bowl, then

took the pot of boiling water off the stove and poured it over the ingredients. She put it on the kitchen table while it steeped, and sat watching the wisps of steam swirl up into the air and disappear. She knew the recipe off by heart, having studied it carefully over the last few days. It was one they'd never had to use, for which she was truly glad.

She checked the clock on the wall, then poured the concoction into a porcelain cup, straining it in a finely meshed sieve. She stared at the brew, then, before she could change her mind, picked up the cup and drank, not stopping until she'd finished it all.

Sara threw away the soggy mass of herbs and washed the cup, bowl and sieve thoroughly so that no one would know what she'd done. She replaced the jars in the pantry, then selected a novel from the bookcase and sat in an armchair to read.

The words merged into each other, her mind too full of other thoughts to concentrate on the book. Here, on a pallet on the floor, was where Cassandra had died only a month earlier, her broken ribs having perforated her lungs. Sara hadn't been able to do anything to help her, only give her herbal drinks to alleviate the pain, and hold her hand so she wasn't alone when she passed. Anna-Maria had sung her song to help her soul find its way; she could only hope that Cassandra had found peace, wherever she was.

Rosa had gone to the village to call the priest and organise the collection of Cassandra's body. Instead, Sara had taken Anna-Maria to the grave in the clearing in the woods.

'His soul is still here,' the old woman had said, her eyes glazing over as she turned, searching. 'As is that of the boy.' She shuddered. 'There is much evil here. I must send Lapo's soul away if Bob is to rest in peace once more.'

While she carried out the ritual, Sara had gone a little further into the woods and dug a hole with the shovel she had brought. The ground was damp beneath the layers of rotting foliage, and the soft peaty soil had been easy to dig. By the time Anna-Maria finished, the hole was ready.

Sara took hold of Lapo under his arms and pulled him off the grave, trying not to grimace at the feel of his skin and the smell coming off his body. His shirt was encrusted with dried blood, but there was no trace of the pool of blood that had been underneath him. She lost no time in wondering, however, but dragged him across the clearing to the hole she'd prepared. It seemed to take forever; she had to keep stopping to wipe the sweat from her eyes and catch her breath, before bending over to drag him again. Time slowed down, and she carried out her task in silence, her grunts the only sounds in the clearing.

His body made a dull thud as it fell into the hole. Sara turned her head and wept. She wept not only for herself, but for the man she'd had to bury, a man who could have been so much, if only he'd been able to overcome his past.

'His soul is gone,' Anna-Maria said, her hand on Sara's arm. 'Finish now, so we can leave his mortal body to spend eternity here.'

Sara picked up the shovel and filled in the hole, refusing to think about what she was doing. She'd wanted to tell someone, but Rosa and Anna-Maria had vehemently insisted she couldn't.

'You're already regarded as a witch by some. Do you really want to be condemned without a trial?' Anna-Maria had said, her blue eyes watery with tears.

'But I killed him!' she'd exclaimed. She'd been able to think of nothing else, reliving the moment the knife had slid into his body over and over again, until she thought she'd go mad.

'He was attacking you. You weren't to blame.' Rosa had implored her to listen to Anna-Maria and eventually Sara had agreed, but she knew she would carry the guilt to her dying day.

She'd covered Lapo's grave with fallen leaves and

undergrowth. As she finished, the dragonfly flew over and came to rest on the handle of the shovel. It was the first time she'd seen it since Lapo had shown up. She watched it in silence for a while, its presence calming her, until Anna-Maria had told her it was time they returned to the cottage. Sara had brooded over that fateful day ever since, her heart heavy with sorrow.

❧

Rosa chattered non-stop while she took the items she'd brought back from the village out of the basket. Sara half listened, uninterested in local gossip. The first cramp hit her as she picked up a loaf of bread to put away.

'You don't look very well.' Rosa took the bread from her. 'Go and lie down, you're as white as a sheet.'

'I think I will.'

Sara somehow made it up the stairs, clutching her stomach as more cramps struck. She took a few old towels from the cupboard on the landing and spread them over her bed before lying down. She closed her eyes and prayed it would be over soon.

She tossed and turned all afternoon, muttering in her sleep as strange dreams assailed her. Faces appeared then faded away, women she had never seen before but felt as if she'd known all her life, clothed differently but all with the same air about them, that reminded her of the Grove. They told her stories, about their lives, about the dragonflies, about the curse that tainted the land, and their work as healers, their voices fading and growing louder as they talked over each other. She tried to tell them about Lapo, and the baby, becoming agitated as her voice was lost among theirs. And then *She* arrived, the Healer. The others quieted as She spoke, her soft words and gentle manner calming Sara, absolving her of her past, giving her hope for the future.

❧

When she awoke, Sara couldn't remember anything of the Healer's discourse, except for her parting words: 'This was not the right time for the next healer. The circle will turn and the time will come again, and when it does, you will know.'

Still half asleep, Sara vowed to trust her instincts in the future. She had ignored the lack of dragonflies at the Grove, the empty bushes and plants that would normally be covered in the jewel-coloured insects, and had let herself be led astray, with disastrous consequences. It would never happen again.

She took the bloodied towels off the bed and changed her stained nightdress, then bundled everything up in an old sheet and carried it downstairs. Rosa followed her as she went out into the garden, and said nothing when Sara took a match and set fire to the bundle. But as they stood together, watching the flames devour the material, the old serving woman put her arm around Sara's shoulders and held her tight.

33

MARCH 1900

S ara popped her head round the door, the tavern's interior
gloomy after the bright sunshine outside.

'Good morning, Dorotea. I've brought that cream you asked me for.'

'Sara. Come in, come in!' The little woman bustled over from behind the bar, brushing wisps of hair away from her face. She greeted Sara with a hug. 'Thank goodness. My back's been playing up again, ever since that rain we had last week.'

'This will set you right. Rub it in at least twice a day, more if you can, and you'll feel better in a few days. Bernardo swore by it.' Sara handed her the pot.

Dorotea unscrewed it and took a deep sniff. 'Ooh, that smells lovely. Gregorio will think it's his lucky night tonight!' She gave a lewd wink and chuckled loudly.

Sara giggled. Over the years she'd struck up a warm friendship with Dorotea, and often dropped in during her rounds for a coffee and a chat. She was slightly in awe of Dorotea's husband, Gregorio. He was a huge bear of a man in his late fifties with a bushy black beard and fearsome eyebrows, usually set in a frown. He managed to lumber from the beer tap to his favourite armchair set by the fireplace in the bar, where he spent hours talking to customers about how he would set the world to rights, while his wife dashed about keeping the inn running.

'Glad to help, it's all part of the service.' Sara picked up her basket, pocketing the coins Dorotea had given her.

'Have you got others to see today?' her friend asked.

'No, you're the last. I'm going to drop in on Anna-Maria, she wasn't feeling too good yesterday. I'd like to check how she's doing.'

'Yes, you look after her. What would we do without our soul catcher? Who's going to take care of the Hanging Tree once she's gone?' Dorotea mused.

Sara hid a smile. Since she had become a healer, assisted by Anna-Maria, the old woman had gone up in the villagers' esteem. They no longer laughed at her and whispered behind her back; instead, she had become someone they listened to when asking for advice.

'You go and sit yourself down while I get you a coffee and a piece of cake. We can't have you fading away, otherwise what'll we do? Look at you, all skin and bone.' Dorotea ignored Sara's protests and guided her over to a table. 'There's only you and our guest in, anyway, it'll give me something to do.'

Sara glanced over at the table in the corner. She hadn't noticed the man sitting there in the gloom, reading a newspaper. He looked up and nodded at them, then stood and made his way over.

'I didn't want to interrupt,' he said. 'Ivano Fabbri, pleased to meet you.'

Sara shook his outstretched hand, his grip pleasantly firm. 'I'm Sara Innocenti, the pleasure's mine.'

'Sit yourself down,' Dorotea said, 'and I'll bring you over a coffee, too, Signor Fabbri.'

'Do you mind?'

Sara gestured to him to take a seat. 'Your accent's not from here.'

'No.' He rested his elbows on the table and leaned towards her. 'I like to travel, I get bored staying in one place for too long. I find work wherever I end up, stay for a while, then move on when I feel restless.'

'And what brings you to Gallicano?' Sara was intrigued by this man. His skin had the tanned, weathered texture of someone used to working outdoors, and his short black hair was roughly trimmed, as if he'd done it himself. His brown eyes were the same shade as Bernardo's, and she felt a sudden pang of nostalgia. Ivano seemed the same kind of man: relaxed, at ease with himself and the world, shirt sleeves rolled up, ready for whatever the day would bring. She hadn't been interested in anyone since her experience with Lapo, although many had tried to win her affection, but she found herself drawn to the man in front of her.

He shrugged. 'I followed my feet, and they led me here. I don't suppose you know if there's any work about? I'll do anything, from plumbing to fixing broken doors to painting. I was going to ask around the village later on, but you seem to know everyone around here. Or perhaps you need someone?'

Sara opened her mouth to answer, but was interrupted by Dorotea placing a tray on the table between them.

'Here you go. This'll set you up for the day.' She laughed heartily. 'There's a selection of cakes, take whatever you like. I would join you, but I'd better get the stew on for our lunchtime customers.' She scuttled off into the kitchen, closing the door behind her.

Sara reached over and picked up a coffee. She added some sugar and slowly stirred, the liquid so dense the spoon could almost stand up in it. 'Dorotea's coffee is the strongest I've ever tasted, be warned,' she said as Ivano stared at his cup.

'I can see that,' he said, taking a cautious sip. His face screwed up at the strong, bitter taste, making Sara laugh.

'You'll get used to it.' She picked up a piece of apricot tart and bit into it, closing her eyes in ecstasy. 'This, on the other hand, is pure heaven. Here, try a piece.'

Ivano took the other slice and tasted it. 'Mmm, I see what you mean. Does she make it herself?'

'Yes. She's an excellent cook.'

'Apart from coffee.' He grinned at her. 'So, as I was saying, do you know of any work?'

'You could try the farms, they always need labourers, especially this time of year.'

'What about a handyman? Do you have anything that needs fixing?'

Sara choked on her cake, coughing until it passed. 'Sorry. I live in an old cottage in the middle of the woods, everything needs fixing! My grandfather used to do it, but since he passed, Rosa and I have been trying to keep up with things. It's not easy, you know.' For some reason, she felt as if she should justify herself. 'We're healers, we cure people. We're busy all day long, what with the Grove, making our remedies for the villagers, keeping the cottage clean and tidy, and visiting those patients who can't come to us. By the time evening comes, we're shattered. We usually fall asleep in front of the fire.'

'Maybe I could come and take a look, fix the worst of it,' Ivano suggested.

'I-I don't have money to pay you,' Sara said, crestfallen.

'A room to sleep and food in my belly is more than enough payment for me. I can always work in the fields to earn some money.'

Sara brightened. 'That I can give you.'

'Then we have a deal.' Ivano held out his hand and she shook it, noticing that he kept hold of her hand a little longer than was necessary.

'Before we go up to the cottage, I want to check if Anna-Maria's all right,' Sara said as they left the tavern.

'Who's she?'

'Gallicano's soul catcher.'

'I won't ask.' Ivano put his hands in his pockets and walked quietly beside her. She appreciated his silence, it gave her the chance to try to reorder the thoughts whirling around her head. His presence distracted her from everything else, all she could concentrate on was her attraction to this mysterious man. She knew nothing about him, but felt as though she'd known him since the beginning of time.

'That's quite a tree,' he remarked as they rounded the curve in the road, his surprised tone breaking the quiet around them.

'That's the Hanging Tree,' Sara whispered, avoiding looking at its branches. The memory of her parents dangling lifelessly from it was as fresh in her mind as the day it had happened so many years before. Their distorted faces still haunted her dreams at night.

Ivano shuddered. 'I wouldn't like to live in that cottage.'

'That's Anna-Maria's place,' Sara said with a grim smile.

'Now I understand why she's called the soul catcher.' They stopped beneath the tree. He placed his hand on the trunk and looked up into its branches. 'It feels like something bad happened here.'

'Many bad things have happened here, that's why we need Anna-Maria. She guides the souls to their resting place.'

'She must be a remarkable woman.'

'She is.'

Sara poked her head round the cottage door, her eyes adjusting to the gloomy interior. 'Anna-Maria,' she called, her voice echoing around the empty room. She pushed the door wide open, letting the sunlight stream in. Dust motes hung suspended in the beam, glittery specks that danced in the air.

'Maybe she's round the back,' Sara said, returning to Ivano, who was still standing on the doorstep.

The vegetable patch was empty, and Sara looked around, bewildered. 'Where can she be? Yesterday I told her to stay in bed if she didn't feel well, she can't have gone far.' A sudden thought struck her and she ran down the path she'd walked only once in her life.

The wooden fence was more rickety than ever, the ivy thicker than before, tendrils sneaking along the ground towards the nearest tree. The gate was open, hanging drunkenly on its rusted hinges. Sara burst through and stopped.

'Anna-Maria,' she called, relieved.

The old woman turned to her, an irritated look on her face. 'What's the matter? Can't a person take five minutes to themselves without the world falling apart?'

'I'm sorry. I checked the cottage but you weren't there, nor in the garden. I thought...' Sara's voice broke.

Anna-Maria's face softened. 'You thought I'd died,' she said, less harshly this time. 'As you can see, I'm alive and well. I sometimes come here to contemplate. I find it soothing, the spirits keep me company.' She walked over to them, wincing in pain from her stiff limbs. 'Who's this, then? Aren't you going to introduce us?' She looked Ivano up and down, her keen eyes missing nothing.

'Yes, of course,' Sara said, flustered. 'This is Ivano, he's going to be staying at the cottage for a while, giving us a hand. Ivano, this is Anna-Maria.'

He held out his hand. 'Sara's told me so much about you, it's an honour to meet you.'

Anna-Maria snorted. 'I dread to think what she's said!' Her eyes twinkled as she winked at Sara. 'It looks like you've got yourself a good one. It's about time, child.'

Sara wanted the ground to swallow her up. 'He's here to do some odd jobs, Anna-Maria. Nothing more.'

'We'll see.' The old woman chuckled. 'Come on, then. Seeing as you've disturbed my peace and quiet, we might as well go and get a cup of tea.'

'She's quite a character,' Ivano said as they left the village and headed up the road towards the cottage. 'That was an interesting couple of hours.'

'She may seem tough on the outside, but she's got a heart of gold. Now you'll meet Rosa – she lives with me and helps prepare all the remedies.'

'You mentioned her. Is she anything like Anna-Maria?'

'No, she's the exact opposite. But no less tough,' Sara added.

'I consider myself warned.' Ivano's laugh was deep and warm, touching a spot inside her she'd kept hidden all these years and melting the icy barrier she'd created. She gripped her basket tighter and wondered what the future held for her.

As they crossed the clearing, the dragonfly appeared and flitted around their heads, darting between them.

'She's beautiful.' Ivano stopped and admired the insect.

'He.'

'What?' His head turned as he followed the dragonfly's flight.

'Nothing.' Sara blushed. Nobody knew she communicated with the dragonflies in the Grove, and she wanted to keep it that way. The villagers accepted her as a healer, but if they should think she was crazy... The memory of her parents' behaviour was still fresh in the locals' minds, and she shuddered at the thought of what they could do to her.

'It's gone.' Ivano sounded disappointed.

'Don't worry, it'll be back,' Sara promised. 'And there are hundreds of them in the Grove, I'll show you later.' Her pace quickened as her heart sang with the dragonfly's promise of love and hope for the future.

34

APRIL 1900

S ara could see Rosa watching them from the back doorstep, arms folded across her chest in disapproval. Irritated, she turned and flashed a bright smile at Ivano, who was busy mending a hole in the fence around the chicken coop.

'Thanks for everything you're doing. We really appreciate it. The cottage is looking much better now.'

He stood up and stretched, his shirt lifting so she could see his taut stomach muscles. She lowered her gaze, embarrassed at the thoughts going through her head. He'd been staying at the cottage almost a month, and their daily conversations had soon turned into light flirting. But nothing had happened between them. Yet. The dragonfly's promise grew more insistent with each day that passed, but somehow she found it impossible to act on it.

'It's a pleasure. I've got a soft bed to sleep in at night, and good food in my stomach during the day. What more could I want?' He winked at her and patted his belly.

Sara swallowed nervously. Rosa had had words with her only the day before, telling her in no uncertain terms what she would think of her if anything happened with Ivano. In the end,

Sara had stormed off before she said something she would regret. She'd thrown herself on her bed and given in to her angry tears, sobbing in frustration. She wasn't getting any younger, and if she wasn't careful, she truly would be the last of the healers.

Her experience with Lapo had taught her to be cautious, and she cared for no man in the village, but she was aware that time was running out. Sara wanted her daughter to be created from a loving union, not some quick fumble with a local. She thought of her grandmother and Bernardo, how their love had endured beyond death, and knew she would accept nothing less.

'I've found work in the fields too, like you suggested, so I'll be around for a couple more months,' he said, interrupting her thoughts. 'I'll probably stay until June, when planting's finished, then move on to pastures new.' He nudged her, clearly pleased with his pun.

She gave a strained smile. 'You won't stay until harvest?'

'No, I'll be long gone before then. I told you, I'm a restless spirit. I never stay in one place very long. I love being here in the mountains, but I can already hear the sea calling to me. After that, who knows? Maybe Rome, I've always wanted to go there.' He glanced at her, then reached over and touched her arm. 'Don't worry, I'll make sure the cottage is in good shape before I go.'

'Thank you. I'll leave you to finish here.' Sara made her way over to the Grove, tears pricking at her eyes. The dragonfly had promised her a future, but it appeared Ivano cared for her only as a friend. Dark, lonely days loomed ahead of her, the image of her daughter playing carefree in the garden fading and vanishing. She opened the gate and went over to the bench Bernardo had made one long winter, carving delicate dragonflies and flowers into the back, which Ivano had moved beneath the apple trees. Blossom fell onto her hair as she sat deep in thought, sadness sapping her energy and her will to do any work.

A shadow fell over her. Sara looked up, sure it was Rosa come to continue her tirade, and braced herself for the impending fight. Dazed, she gave a shaky smile as Ivano took hold of her hands and pulled her to her feet. He leaned over and touched her forehead with his, then his mouth found hers. He kissed her hard, full of desire, only stopping to draw breath. She gasped.

He shook his head. 'Don't say anything,' he said, his voice low and husky. He wrapped his arms around her and kissed her again, and they both sank to the ground. She moaned as he lifted her dress, his hands roaming over her body, heat flushing her skin. She put her hands under his shirt, running her fingertips over his back and shoulders, then lower, daring to slide her hands beneath the waist of his trousers. He gave a deep groan, shifting so she could take hold of him and feel his need for her. He quickly knelt and flung off his clothes, his eyes never leaving her face as she lay before him on the ground. Their breath came fast as he pulled her dress over her head, and then they forgot everything else as their bodies touched and desire took over.

Afterwards, they lay side by side in peaceful bliss, his fingers making her skin tingle as they ran over her body. Sara felt as though she'd always belonged in his arms. She finally felt safe.

'Why did you come to me?' She was warm and drowsy in the midday sun, her body quiet and sated even though her mind was a jumble of thoughts.

'The dragonfly.'

She turned to face him, her eyebrows raised.

'Don't look at me like that.' He gave an embarrassed laugh. 'As I watched you walk away, the dragonfly flew in my face like it was attacking me.' He paused. 'I swear I heard it say, "Go after her before it's too late". Now you're going to think I'm crazy and wish you'd never met me.'

'Not at all. I believe you.' Sara placed her hand on the soft downy hair on his chest. 'So many strange things happen around here, I believe anything by now.' She rested her head on the ground, sighing with contentment.

'I won't stay, you know that,' Ivano said, stroking her hair.

'Yes, I know.' Sara's heart broke, but she knew she wouldn't try to make him stay.

'I can't promise you anything, but I will come back, if I can.'

'I don't need any promises. This is more than enough.' At that moment, she could accept that he would abandon her, knowing that he had left her the most precious gift of all. The next healer.

When Rosa caught Ivano slipping out of Sara's room in the early hours a couple of weeks later, she reacted exactly as Sara had dreaded she would. Ivano sat perched on the edge of an armchair, shame-faced, while Rosa ranted about their disgusting behaviour, and how disappointed she was.

'What if she's with child?' she yelled, pointing a trembling finger at Ivano. 'Did you think about that? No, all you men think about is having your fun, then running off without a care in the world and leaving the woman to deal with all the rest. Sara is the daughter of a contessa, not some backstreet trollop!'

Ivano jerked, clearly shocked. 'You're a contessa?'

'No, I'm not,' Sara said firmly. 'That is, my mother was, but I renounced my title and everything that goes with it. For goodness' sake, Rosa, I'm thirty-six, not some innocent little girl being seduced. I know what I'm doing.'

Rosa glared at them both, her chest heaving. 'You'll regret this, mark my words. He'll leave you, they always do, and then what'll you do? Nobody will have you after this.'

'I don't want a husband, Rosa, I thought that was obvious. Otherwise I'd be married with an enormous brood of children by now. Please, you're embarrassing me and you're embarrassing Ivano. We're both adults, we know what we're doing.'

'Pah.' Rosa stormed back off upstairs.

Sara glanced at Ivano, not knowing whether to laugh or cry. His unconstrained snort made her burst into giggles.

'She's right about one thing, though,' Ivano said eventually, trying to hold back more laughter.

'What's that?'

'You could be with child.' His voice was serious.

'Ivano...' Sara didn't know what to say.

'I know I said I'm a free spirit, but I won't leave you on your own if you are.'

'I'm not.'

'How can you be sure?' he insisted.

'I just know.' She hated herself for lying, but she wouldn't use the excuse of being with child to make him stay.

'I've never loved anyone before, but you're special to me.' He kissed her gently.

'I won't force you to give up your freedom for me, you'll only resent me for it,' Sara said, pulling away, desperately trying not to show him how she really felt. 'And anyway, I'm a healer, it will always be the most important thing in my life.'

He sat back, making himself comfortable. 'Tell me about your family, and the healers.'

So she did.

35

Sara's moans echoed through the cottage as the contractions got closer together. Rosa sat beside her, murmuring words of encouragement. Outside, the snow fell with a quiet, shushing sound, all noise muffled by the white blanket.

'You're doing really well, we're almost there,' Rosa said. There was a sudden flash of colour outside the window. 'Your little friend has come to see if you're all right, look.'

Sara turned her head and smiled at the dragonfly resting on the windowsill, a splash of bright blue against the white background. 'He came.' She lay her head back on the pillow, grateful for a moment's relief from the pain.

When the next contraction arrived, she looked again at the dragonfly, letting her mind be drawn into the depths of its black eyes. The pain receded as her mind floated free of her body, flitting over the snow-covered ground beside the dragonfly. She gasped as they soared high into the sky, familiar sights disappearing behind them as they journeyed further into the mountains. Rivers, lakes, trees all came and went, the mountain peaks lost in the curtain of cloud, and still they went higher. Wisps of grey mist surrounded them, and then they burst through the clouds into bright sunlight. Below, the white peaks sparkled and glittered as if diamonds had been scattered over the snow. Sara lost herself to the exhilaration of it all, carefree and weightless, carried along by the currents to wherever they wished to take her.

A piercing cry brought her back down to earth, her mind again reunited with her body. A soothing calm washed over her, and she opened her eyes to see Rosa gently wiping a small bundle in her arms. The bundle shook, and another loud cry filled the room, more insistent this time.

'She sounds hungry,' Rosa said with a laugh.

'She?' Sara whispered, her throat dry after the long labour.

'Yes, you've got a daughter.' Rosa's eyes filled with tears as she passed the bundle to Sara. 'Here. She's beautiful.'

Sara looked down at the pink face peering at her from the blanket, blue eyes moving restlessly as they tried to focus on this strange new world her daughter found herself in. *Her daughter!* Sara's heart filled with love as she watched the baby latch onto her breast, and she knew she would never have room for anyone else from then on.

She could hear Rosa moving quietly around the room, tidying up, and Sara was glad to be alone with her thoughts. Memories of the day Ivano had left surfaced, and she let them in.

'If I go now, maybe I can get work on a ship before the winter sets in,' he said to her. They were lying beneath the apple tree in the Grove, Sara with her head on Ivano's shoulder and an arm draped across his stomach. He played with a lock of her hair, twisting it around his finger.

'A ship?'

'I thought a change of scenery would do me good.' He smiled at her, but his eyes were sad.

Sara squashed the emotions threatening to burst through

her chest, her heart heavy. 'I won't marry you, Ivano, and you know why.'

They had talked about it many times since Rosa's outburst. Ivano was worried he'd ruined Sara's reputation ('What reputation?' she'd asked wryly), while Sara was adamant she would never get married, not after everything she'd been through with her own parents. But she'd never told him it was because she loved him too much, too deeply, because she wouldn't be able to bear it if he knew, and he left her anyway. There was a burning desire within him to travel the world, and she knew that he would come to resent both her and the baby if she forced him to stay. She tried to fight her feelings for him, but it was useless. She loved him with all her soul.

'I know you're with child.'

Sara froze. 'How?'

'I just do. Were you going to tell me?'

'I...' She lowered her eyes, unable to look at him.

'It's all right, I understand. You need a healer to carry on your work, and I was able to give you what you wanted.' A bitter tone crept into his voice. 'I hope it's a girl, otherwise it will all have been for nothing.'

'Don't.'

'Why not? That's all I am to you, isn't it?' His eyes blazed with anger as he looked at her.

'No.' She wriggled out of his arms and sat up. 'Whether you believe it or not, I care for you. You're the first man I've ever had feelings for, and you'll be the last. I-I hope that one day you'll find your way back to me.' She hung her head, regretting her last words, hoping that he hadn't heard the longing in her voice.

He'd pulled her to him then and kissed her with a fierce passion, crushing her against his body as if he'd never let go. She'd hugged him back, clinging on to him, breathing in his scent, impressing his image on her mind.

That evening, he'd said his goodbyes and left the cottage, not looking back as he crossed the clearing and disappeared into the woods. Sara had stood watching from the door, her heart breaking as he walked out of her life.

Tears rolled down Sara's cheeks as she thought of Ivano and how he should be there with her, on this day. She stroked her daughter's soft hair, the child fast asleep after sating her hunger. A movement in the shadows caught her eye, and she smiled, content that Ginevra and Bernardo were there as well, watching over her.

'Have you got a name?' Rosa asked quietly.

Sara jumped. She'd forgotten Rosa was there. 'Emilia,' she replied. Ivano's mother's name.

'You know, I understand why you did what you did,' Rosa said. 'Ivano was a good man, better than many from around here. And now we have the next healer.' She looked fondly at the sleeping baby. 'And for what it's worth, I think you were right not to marry him.'

Sara stared, open-mouthed, as Rosa got up.

'I'll bring you a tea and something to eat,' she said as she walked over to the door.

Sara shook her head in disbelief. 'Wonders will never cease.' The baby shifted and emitted a loud burp, and Sara burst out laughing. 'I'm going to enjoy getting to know you, my little dragonfly in winter,' she whispered, wiping the tears from her eyes.

Anna-Maria sat in the armchair by the fire, the baby snugly wrapped up in her arms. Sara sat opposite her, taking a well-earned break.

'She kept me up all night, now look at her. Little Miss Butter-wouldn't-melt,' Sara complained.

'Ha, they know who they can take advantage of, without a doubt,' Anna-Maria said, gazing down at the sleeping baby. 'She's going to be quite a character, just like her mother.'

'That's for sure.' Rosa handed Sara a cup of tea. 'I put an extra spoon of honey in it, you look like you need the energy.'

Sara took a sip and grimaced. 'It's a bit sweet.'

'Drink it up, it'll help you get through the day,' Anna-Maria ordered.

Sara would have preferred a coffee, but kept quiet. She secretly enjoyed having all this fuss made of her, especially after the night she'd had.

'So, we have our healer for the next generation.' Anna-Maria stroked the baby's cheek with a gnarled, calloused finger. 'Little Emilia. Thank goodness. For a while there, I thought you would be the last. At least I can die in peace now.'

Sara almost spat out her mouthful of tea. 'Anna-Maria! Don't say those things!'

'Why not? I'm ninety-seven, no one lives forever. Not even me.'

'Yes, but you can't leave me! Not now.' Sara put down the cup, her hand trembling. The thought terrified her.

'Child, like a tree knows when to shed its leaves for its winter slumber, so my body knows when it's time for me to depart this world. I can feel the signs, it won't be long now.'

'But the Hanging Tree and the souls, who will take care of them?'

Anna-Maria frowned as Emilia gave a squawk and shushed the baby, gently rocking her in her arms. 'The spirits are at peace, I haven't been idle all these years. Those who could move on have done so, the others are no longer wandering in limbo, waiting for someone to guide them. My work is done, there is no more need for a soul catcher. I have decided that the tree will be cut down. No one else will die on its branches.'

Sara knelt by Anna-Maria's side. 'Please don't leave me.'

'You have Rosa to look after you, you aren't alone,' the old woman said, reaching over and caressing Sara's hair. 'And when you have finished the work you were placed on this earth to do, we will find each other again.'

'I can't...' Tears rolled down Sara's cheeks.

'You will find the way. We women always do,' Anna-Maria said gently. 'It's what we do best.'

36

The two girls worked side by side in the Grove, laughing and chatting as they removed the weeds from around the plants. Sara couldn't help wondering where the years had gone. It seemed only yesterday Emilia had been born; now she was thirteen years old, not quite a woman, no longer a child. She was a firm favourite with the villagers who came to the cottage for their remedies, endearing herself to old and young alike. Sara had noticed the local boys glancing at her, trying to hide their blushing cheeks, and couldn't help smiling at their awkward attempts to talk to her. Chiara was quieter, preferring to hide behind her stepsister's more vivacious personality, but she had her own fair share of admirers as well.

The family had changed over the years. Anna-Maria's death after Emilia was born had hit her and Rosa hard; they missed the old woman's dry comments and down-to-earth attitude. The Hanging Tree had been chopped down a few days later, another permanent reminder that she was no longer with them. Sara was relieved it was gone, but at the same time she felt that a part of her past had disappeared, and was sad that it would remain only in her memories for as long as she was alive.

Sara kept an eye on the girls, making sure they didn't pull out any young seedlings by mistake. Emilia was quick to learn, understanding instinctively which plants would be best for the villagers' various complaints, while Chiara was happier to stand back and assist whenever she could.

Sara supposed it was only natural; after all, you had to be born a healer, you couldn't become one. Chiara had arrived in their family a year after Emilia, a pink, squalling bundle whose mother had died while giving birth. The father already had five other children to look after, and Sara still remembered the despair on his face when she'd told him of his wife's death. She'd held Chiara out to him, wrapped up in a blanket, the baby's face still smeared with blood, and he'd turned from her. 'Take it away and drown it,' he'd said, trying to hold back his tears. 'I can't look after the ones I've already got, what am I supposed to do with this one as well?' Sara had tried to insist but he'd refused, getting angrier the more she spoke. 'You take it if you bloody want it,' he'd shouted in the end. So she had.

Rosa had reacted precisely as she'd expected; whispering angrily as Sara had stood before her with the baby sleeping in her arms, asking her what on earth had possessed her to take on another woman's child, until she'd leaned over and taken Chiara in her arms. Then her face had softened, and she'd hummed a quiet lullaby as the baby snuffled in its sleep.

'You'll be the death of me, Sara Innocenti,' she'd grumbled. 'But I suppose you couldn't do anything else. Welcome to the family, little one.' She'd glanced up at Sara, her eyes full of tears. 'You did the right thing.'

As Chiara grew up, she followed Rosa everywhere, their bond stronger than any mother and daughter. They adored each other, and Sara was amused to see how Chiara wrapped Rosa around her little finger. No longer the stern woman she'd once been, striking fear into everyone's heart, Rosa was often to be found crawling around the floor on all fours with Chiara on her back yelling, 'Go, horsey, go.'

Emilia was smitten with her new sister, and spent hours playing with her. They grew closer as they got older, plaiting each other's hair and wearing identical clothes, and inventing their own language as they talked about anything and everything. Sara often complained her ears would fall off with all their chatter, but she loved the fact that the cottage was full of life and laughter.

Chiara had been devastated when Rosa died a few months earlier, in March. She'd cried for days, inconsolable.

'Tell her about Anna-Maria, Mamma,' Emilia had begged her one day, unable to bear seeing her sister so upset.

Sara had sat them down. 'Anna-Maria was a dear friend of mine, and of Rosa's. She lived in the cottage next to where the Hanging Tree used to be.' The two girls nodded, Chiara sniffing noisily. 'When Emilia was born, she told me that her time here was almost up, now her work was done. She knew she was going to die, but she was at peace with herself and the world. She'd done everything she'd been put here to do, and knew the time was right. I was so upset, like you, Chiara.' She reached out and stroked the girl's hand. 'I begged her to stay, I couldn't see how I was going to live without her. But of course, I did. It was hard at first, and I cried many tears, just like you. But every day gets a little easier, so little that at first you don't notice it, until all of a sudden you no longer cry when you think of them but smile, and you let those happy memories you tried to shut out back into your heart, where they belong. Rosa will always be with you, as Anna-Maria is always with me, and our lives are all the richer for having known them.'

It must have helped, Sara thought as she watched the two of them. Chiara had stopped crying and gradually returned to her normal, cheerful self, the cottage full of their laughter. Today she seemed calmer, more at peace with the world.

'Mamma, look at the dragonflies,' Emilia called, standing up and stretching her back.

Sara looked over to where Emilia was pointing with her trowel, and her eyes opened wide in surprise. A cloud of dragonflies rose from the fountain, swooping and swirling, their bright colours glinting in the sun as they formed intricate patterns in the air. Sara joined the two girls and the three of them watched the insects' performance, spellbound.

'What are they doing?' Emilia whispered.

'I've no idea,' Sara replied. 'I've never seen them do this, not in all the years I've been here.'

'They're doing it for me,' Chiara said, her voice shaking with emotion.

Sara and Emilia turned and stared at her.

'It's true,' she said defiantly. 'I spoke with the dragonfly this morning, when I went down to collect the eggs, and asked it to prove to me that Rosa is still with us.'

'You spoke with the dragonfly?' Sara said.

'You always do it, so I thought I would too.' Chiara's eyes filled with tears. 'Sometimes it feels like Rosa's still here, with me... I imagine I can almost hear her speaking, if I listen hard enough. So I asked the dragonfly to give me a sign. I know you won't believe me.'

Sara put her arm around the girl's shoulders. 'I believe you. I have seen many unbelievable things in my lifetime, and I too feel the presence here of people I've loved, including Rosa.'

'So do I.' Emilia put her arm around Chiara as well. 'I'm glad she's still around, keeping an eye on us.'

Sara's gaze followed the dragonflies' tireless dance. 'I always knew there was magic in this place,' she whispered.

❧

She hadn't known at the time, but those were the last months of happiness they would have for a while. There had been rumours of an imminent war, which proved to be true by the end of July. For a time the Italian people could rest easy, watching from the sidelines as Italy remained neutral, but their peace of mind didn't last long.

Italy entered the war in the spring of 1915, and families all over the country watched their world fall apart. For Sara, life at the cottage carried on as normal, but she secretly held on to the small spark of hope that one day Ivano would come back and they could be together once more.

37

S ara stood by the front door, holding the letter the postman had delivered. She could still hear him whistling as he cycled down the road back to the village. It hadn't yet snowed, but the air was cold and piercing, and a light frost dusted the trees. Behind her, Emilia and her new husband, Sebastiano, were talking as they made breakfast together, soft laughter spilling through the quiet cottage.

'Mamma, it's ready,' Emilia called.

Sara made no reply, her eyes fixed on the envelope in her hands. Who had sent it? The postmark was illegible, although it had an Italian stamp. *Was it...?* Her heart leaped, and she felt faint. *After all these years?*

'Mamma! You'll catch your death. Come back inside.' Emilia bustled past her and closed the door, shutting out the chilly morning air. 'Look at you, you're shivering.' She pulled Sara's shawl tighter around her shoulders and rubbed her back, then stopped and took a closer look. 'Is everything all right? What's that?'

'I... A letter.' Sara waved her away, irritated. 'I didn't realise I had to answer to my daughter now.'

Emilia stepped back, a hurt look on her face. 'I was worried, that's all. It's not like you to let the cold into the house.' She attempted a smile.

'I'm sorry.' Sara felt guilty. After all, Emilia had insisted she remain with them at the house after she'd married, even though Sara had offered to leave. She remembered the conversation well, and the horrified look on Emilia's face when Sara had told her she would go and live in Anna-Maria's cottage.

'No!'

'But it's empty, no one's used it for years. She left it to me, and now you're married it's about time I let you get on with your life.'

'Not there. No. And besides, it's probably full of mould and damp from being empty for so long.'

'That can soon be fixed. The Hanging Tree has been cut down, the souls are long gone, if that's what you're worried about. It's not a bad place...'

'I know, bad things happened there.' Emilia sighed. 'That may be so, but I get goosebumps every time I walk past that house, it gives me the creeps. There's no way I'm going to let you live there alone. You're staying here, and that's final!'

Sara had been surprised by her daughter's insistence and given in. She was glad she'd stayed, although she'd regretted it a few times since then, in particular when she craved some peace from the confusion around her. Like now.

'I got this letter. I've no idea who it's from.'

Emilia's expression softened. 'Do you think it's my father?'

Sara shrugged. 'I wouldn't think so. But...'

'But, what if it is?' Emilia hugged her. 'Go upstairs and read it, Mamma. Take as long as you want. Call me if you need anything.'

Sara nodded, and slowly made her way upstairs. Once in her room, she locked the door and sat down on a chair by the window. With shaking hands, she picked up her glasses and rested them on her nose, then read the letter.

Dear Signora Innocenti,

You don't know me. I'm Capitano Paolo D'Angelo and I am a friend of Ivano Fabbri. We served together during the war, and became good friends. He spoke often of you, the cottage in the Tuscan mountains, the Grove, and your dedication to your healing. He loved you deeply, I could see it in his eyes whenever he mentioned your name. I hope this gives you some solace for what follows.

It is with a heavy heart that I must write to you and inform you of his death several days ago. It was our final battle, one that my men courageously faced and fought, even though we were outnumbered from the start. Ivano was a good man, a brave soldier, and when one of our unit fell, shot through the leg, Ivano dashed back to recover him without a thought to his own safety, only to be felled by a stray bullet. I lost many men that day, all of them worth their weight in gold. And just a few hours later, the end of the war was declared. I myself was injured badly, and am now recovering in hospital. I hope to return home in a matter of days, but it will be with much sadness − I may have lost my arm, but the loss of my men hurts me more.

I enclose a letter Ivano wrote for you some time ago and entrusted to my care, should anything happen to him. I hoped never to have to send it to you, but God's will has decided otherwise.

I remain ever your obedient servant,
Paolo D'Angelo.

A single tear ran down Sara's cheek as she read, her vision blurring. She blinked, then put the letter down on the windowsill. The date on the envelope was barely readable − 18 November 1918. Ivano had survived, right until the end. Had he joined up from the beginning? It seemed this captain had known him for some time, so it was likely. The war had affected them all, so many lives lost, so many young men who would never come home. Captain D'Angelo had been one of the lucky ones, although she doubted he considered himself fortunate.

She could see the other envelope inside the first, and wondered if it had the answers to her questions. She lifted it out and held it between her thumb and first finger, her name written in black ink that stood stark against the crisp white paper. For a moment she imagined she could hear the sounds of gunshots, men shouting, loud explosions, and terrified screams, then they faded and she was sitting, trembling, by the window.

She got up, walked over to her bedside table, and put the envelope in the drawer. She closed it firmly, picked up the captain's letter and curled up on her bed, holding it to her chest while she sobbed quietly.

38

'Now, Mamma, make sure you stay indoors today. Sebastiano and I must go down to the village, but it's icy out and we don't want you falling over.' Emilia brought over a blanket and tucked it around Sara's legs.

Sara flapped her hands. 'Oh, get on with you. I may be almost sixty, but I'm not that old and doddery yet. And a bit of snow never hurt anyone. When I was your age–' She broke off, seeing in her mind's eye the bright blue dragonfly at the edge of the wood one winter's day.

'You know the doctor said to take it easy. You've been a bit unsteady on your feet lately, I think you should stay indoors. There's no reason for you to go outside – you can't do any work in the Grove in this weather, and we've fed the animals. So do as you're told for once!' Emilia stood, hands on hips, but with a smile on her face.

'I know you see me as a stubborn old woman, but you're just as bad,' Sara complained. 'Look at you, going outside with that belly.'

Emilia glanced down, putting her hands protectively over

her stomach. 'It's not that big, I'm only five months along. And we'll be careful.'

Sara leaned forward and touched her daughter's stomach, her eyes closed as she concentrated. After a few seconds, she opened them again, a smile on her face. 'You take care of that little girl in there. She's precious, you know.'

'Girl? How can you tell?'

'I just can. You will too, with time.' She sat back and grunted with satisfaction. 'You're carrying the next healer, that's a big responsibility.'

'That's good to hear. But you're my responsibility too, so sit here by the fire and keep warm. That's an order. Use the chamber pot if you need to, don't even think about going to the outhouse.'

'All right,' Sara grudgingly promised.

'If it starts snowing heavily again we'll stop at Chiara's, so we might be late back, but there's plenty of food in the larder if you get hungry. And Sebastiano has stocked up the pile of logs, so don't let the fire go out.'

'I know how to look after myself, I've been doing it for years. Get going, otherwise it'll start snowing and you'll never leave me in peace!' Sara watched as her daughter gathered her bags and got ready to go.

'You'll be all right?' Emilia asked, her face anxious.

'Of course! Now go, Sebastiano's been waiting long enough.'

Sara heard the front door slam and leaned her head against the back of the armchair with a long sigh. She loved her daughter with all her heart, but sometimes she could be tiring. Sara drifted off into a light sleep, snoring softly as the heat from the fire made her drowsy.

❧

She gradually came to a while later, the fire still crackling merrily before her. The room was filled with a white glow, and for an instant she thought her grandmother had come back.

'You foolish woman,' she said, struggling to get out of the armchair. She went over to the window and looked out at the snow falling; large thick flakes, so dense she could barely see the other side of the clearing. 'I suppose that means they won't be back until much later, no way they can walk home in this.'

She sat in the armchair by the window, seeing the snow coating the branches of the trees and making them sag under its weight. It reminded her of that winter long ago, when she first saw the dragonfly in the woods. She relaxed as she watched the hypnotic motion of the falling snowflakes, and her thoughts wandered.

Ghosts of the people she had once known and loved crowded her mind, their faces still as clear as when they'd been alive. Anna-Maria, who'd died almost twenty years earlier at the ripe old age of ninety-seven, was standing beneath the Hanging Tree, her face free of wrinkles and the hardship she'd suffered all her life. Beside her stood a man, looking adoringly at her, and Sara knew she'd returned to her husband's arms after so many years alone.

Rosa, dear, beloved, faithful Rosa, turned and smiled at Sara, her plump figure familiar and reassuring. She wandered about the Grove, trailing her hands over the bushes and plants, a swarm of dragonflies hovering around her. Sara's parents walked behind her, gazing in admiration at the garden.

Bernardo appeared on the back of a dapple-grey mare, and beside him Ginevra, astride a beautiful black stallion. The horse arched its neck and reared, its mane flowing and rippling, and Ginevra laughed as she spoke soothingly to it. The two horses stood side by side, necks arched, while Bernardo and Ginevra waved to Sara. Tears filled her eyes as she saw them holding hands, so in love still, together in death as they could never have been in life.

Cassandra walked behind them, the wild look gone from her eyes, holding hands with her mother. The two looked at peace, and Sara was glad they had found each other again.

Then her heart leapt as she saw Ivano standing before her, chewing nonchalantly on a long piece of straw as he leaned against the wall of the cottage. He was exactly the same as when they'd met, with his short, badly trimmed dark hair, his chin covered with a few days' worth of stubble, his face tanned from working long days in the sun. But instead of a smile, he frowned at her, the twinkle gone from his brown eyes, and then he turned and faded away into nothingness.

Sara came to with a jolt, desperation filling her as she realised she'd lost him. 'Please,' she begged, her voice breaking with emotion. 'I loved you.' She glanced around, and saw that she was inside the cottage, sat in her armchair. Bewildered, she wondered what she had seen. Was it merely her rambling mind, or had she really seen them all? And why was Ivano upset with her?

A sudden thought struck her. *The letter!* It was still upstairs in her bedside table drawer, untouched since she'd put it there more than a year earlier. Trembling, she stood and made her way slowly up the stairs, gripping the banister. She couldn't fall, not now. If she were to find peace, she had to read the letter; she was certain of this.

The drawer was stiff. Her arthritic hands pulled on it with difficulty, and eventually it slid out. The envelope was there, still pristine after all this time. She tutted as she tried to pick it up, her fingers chunky and awkward.

'Got you. To hell with the cold and my arthritis.'

Upstairs it was colder, the heat from the fireplace not having reached up there. She wrapped her shawl more tightly around her and returned downstairs, taking care not to drop the letter. Settled again in her armchair in front of the fire, she pulled the blanket over her knees to warm her chilled bones. Her hands shaking, she opened the envelope.

My darling Sara,

I don't know how to begin this letter. I hope you never have to read it, and I can tell you in person how I feel about you. But this is war, and we never know which day is going to be our last.

I often think back to the day I met you in the tavern in Gallicano, and how my luck changed that day. I was so lonely then, and lost, and for a while you gave me the home life I craved.

I would have given up everything for you back then, settled down and cherished my family. But you were right, and I was wrong. There was still a restlessness in me, a desperate quest for something else, something more, and I would have eventually come to resent you and our child for keeping me there. When I left, I thought it was because you had sent me away – now I realise you were setting me free. I was angry at first, I'm not scared to admit it, but now I have nothing but admiration for you.

I went to the coast and found work on the ships, as I told you I would. And as the years passed, it became more and more difficult to come back to you. Not because I'd changed, but because I was afraid you would have changed. I imagined the woman you'd become, strong and independent, just like Anna-Maria and Rosa, and I was scared you wouldn't want or need me anymore. So, I stayed away, like the coward I am, keeping in my heart the memories of lying entwined in your arms, surrounded by your love and protection.

But this war, it's hard. So many men are dying, young men who should be courting their first love, not lying in agony in a ditch, screaming in pain. The noise, the confusion, the fear, that's what you live with, day in and day out, until you feel as if you'll go mad with it. Two years I've been here, and every day I send a prayer to any god who's listening, begging them to stop this devastation and let us all go home. Home. That is what I consider the cottage, with you and our child, and that is where I want to be, for the rest of my life. I want to lay my head on your breast and hear your heart beating in my ear, and know that I will never have to leave you again.

I must be realistic, though. Any day could be my last – a bomb, a bullet, gas, infection, there are so many ways a man can die out here. And so I write this letter, to give to my captain for safekeeping, and pray that it will make its way to you if I cannot.

Know that I love you, and always will, and I promise you that we will be together again, either in this life or the next.

Yours forever,

Ivano

June 1, 1917

Sara's hands trembled as she read and reread the letter, her world falling apart with every word. Her whole future had been torn away from her by a single bullet finding Ivano in its path. She burst into tears, distraught at the thought of how different her life could have been, the love she had been denied all these years, if only Ivano had been able to quell the wanderlust inside him.

'And you?' she said out loud. 'Could you have turned your back on being a healer for love? Ivano couldn't stay in one place, just as you couldn't have left the cottage and the village behind to go with him.'

She read the last line again. It reminded her of her grandmother and Bernardo, and the dream she'd had while watching the snow. *And what if it hadn't been a dream?* What if Ivano was waiting for her?

The snow was still falling, the late-afternoon sky giving a blue tinge to the wintry scene outside. Sara stood near the window, shivering as a cold draught crept through the frame. A blur crossed the clearing, weaving in and out of the snowflakes, darting backwards and forwards, until the dragonfly came to rest on the windowsill, its delicate wings vibrating gently.

Sara nodded, went over to the back door, and stepped outside. She didn't feel the cold snow seeping through her slippers or the snowflakes melting in her hair and on her shawl. She tucked the letter into her pocket, keeping it gripped tightly between her fingers, and followed the dragonfly down to the Grove.

The gate had been left open, and Sara slipped into the garden, her footsteps muffled in the snow. The dragonfly was resting on the edge of the fountain, like the first time it had led her there, waiting for her to join it. She brushed away some snow and sat beside it, her other hand still on the letter in her pocket.

'It's time, isn't it?' she whispered to the insect. She took a final look around the Grove, satisfied her life's work was over. It would be Emilia's turn now, and her daughter's after her. Warmth flooded her body as her heartbeat slowed, and she closed her eyes, ready for whatever might come.

The darkness around her slowly turned to grey as a white figure came towards her.

'Don't be afraid, Sara,' a voice said, floating across the nothingness.

'Who are you?' Sara thought she'd said the words out loud, but her mouth hadn't opened.

'You know who I am.' The figure came closer, its hands outstretched in friendship.

'I don't...' But she realised she did. 'Yes.' Agnes. The first Healer, the one whose blood ran in her veins, the reason why she had become a healer herself.

'Come. He's waiting.'

Sara took hold of her hand and walked towards her family and her one true love.

❦

A loud cracking sound disturbed the silence. The birds sheltering in the nearby trees rose into the air, cawing and squawking in fear. A cloud of dragonflies hovered over the centuries-old fountain, its marble basin broken cleanly in two. Sara's body was slumped to one side and the letter in her hand quickly became damp in the snow, the ink running across the page until the words were blurred and illegible.

39

The giggling came again, louder this time. Emilia got up out of her armchair, determined to find out who it was.

Leave it.

Emilia sighed. 'I can't, it might be something important.'

I've told you already, it isn't.

Emilia crossed her arms and frowned. 'You don't know everything–'

That's where you're wrong. Don't answer.

Emilia huffed as whoever it was giggled again. She strode over to the door and flung it open. Two boys, about ten years old, stood before her, giggling and nudging each other. Before she could say anything, they ran off down the path and were soon out of sight.

So, who was it?

'Just a couple of children messing around.'

See.

'There's no need to be so smug.' Emilia went to the kitchen and put the kettle on the stove to boil. She busied herself preparing the teapot, then poured the boiling water over the tea leaves and left it to brew. Her mother's voice fell silent, and she didn't know whether to be relieved or sad.

She glanced over at the armchair, half expecting to see Sara sat there. But it was empty as always, just like it had been since that dreadful day they'd found her in the Grove, frozen to death. Emilia had carried the guilt for months afterwards, until her mother had come back from wherever she was and started speaking to her. She'd thought she was going crazy at first, seeing shadows where no shadows should be, and hearing Sara's voice in her head, but she'd come to accept it over time and now she drew comfort from her mother's presence.

'Even though you are an insufferable know-it-all,' she said out loud. She smiled, and sat down at the kitchen table to enjoy her cup of tea.

꙳

Emilia sighed as her four-year-old daughter ran screaming into the house, followed by her three-year-old brother brandishing what looked like a dead rat.

'Mamma, Mamma!' She grabbed on to Emilia's skirts, almost making her fall over. 'Tell him to stop!'

'Give it to me, Giorgio,' Emilia said, holding out her hand. On looking more closely, she saw it *was* a dead rat and changed her mind. 'Take it outside immediately, and go and wash your hands.'

Giorgio looked crestfallen but did as he was told. 'I only wanted to show her, she's such a sissy,' he said as he slammed the door behind him.

Emilia turned and hugged the trembling girl. 'It's gone now.' She sat down and pulled her daughter onto her lap, grunting a little as she made room for her together with her bump. 'You're getting so big, aren't you? All better?'

The little girl nodded and squirmed, trying to get away, her scare already forgotten. 'Can I go outside again, Mamma? I was talking with the dragonflies, until Giorgio found the rat.'

Emilia patted her head. 'Yes, you can go. Tell Giorgio to leave any dead animals he finds alone. And Luisa... have fun with the dragonflies.'

THE END

ACKNOWLEDGEMENTS

When I first started writing about the Innocenti family, I never imagined it would become so popular with readers. The characters have a special place in my heart, and each book has taken me on a wonderful journey. One day I'll go back to Jennifer, Agnese and the family to catch up on their lives, but in the meantime I'm enjoying writing about other healers from the past. My next book will be about Morgana Innocenti – hers is a special story to tell.

Thank you everyone at Bloodhound for helping to make my books the best they can be, and for giving me the possibility to reach new readers all around the world. This has been the busiest year of my life – I can't wait to see what next year brings!

There are many wonderful people who support me on my writing journey, people I've met online who have become good friends, and I'm grateful to every single one of them. Thank you too to everyone who interacts on my Facebook page, or replies to my newsletters – your encouragement helps keep me going. And a shout-out to Skye's Mum and Books, the best readers' group on Facebook!

A special mention goes to my Top Secret Gang members for their support and help, and for reading all my books with such enthusiasm! It's very much appreciated.

Hugs go to Kayleigh and Sarah, for being there whenever I needed them, and for being the two best friends anyone could wish for.

And, last as usual, thank you to my husband, Ivan, for taking care of the everyday chores so I can get on with writing, for understanding when I need some quiet so I can finish that chapter, and for simply being there and believing in me. *Sei l'amore della mia vita per sempre.*

For all the latest news and up-to-date information, you can follow me on:
Facebook
Twitter
Instagram

You can sign up for my newsletter at: https://sendfox.com/lp/1knl41 for up-to-date information on my books, behind the scenes details, chat about life in Italy, and freebies/promos of other authors' books I think you may like.

I only send my newsletter out once a month or so, unless I have any exciting news to share with you!

Printed in Great Britain
by Amazon

61073802R00142